HARD WOOD

LAUREN BLAKELY

COPYRIGHT

Copyright © 2017 by Lauren Blakely, second edition

Cover Design by Qamber Media and Designs. **Sixth Edition 2026**

DEDICATION

This book is dedicated to the readers. To all the wonderful people who picked up Big Rock, or Mister O, or Well Hung, or Full Package, or Joy Ride, or this book. You are the reason Hard Wood is in your hands. Hee hee. Hard Wood in your hands :)

ABOUT

Women often say a good man is hard to find. And a hard man is even better.

That's why I'm quite a catch— good, hard, loaded, and wait for it…I'm ready to settle down too. But the woman I want to pitch my tent with lives clear across the country. Neither of us wants to get lost in those woods. All I have to do is resist her for the week she's in town.

I try. I swear I try. But yeah, that doesn't work out.

And after one fantastic night with my good friend Mia, I'm ready to give her years of nights under the stars. What's a few thousand miles when love's involved? But there's a hitch in my plans — she just hired my adventure tour company. If there's one thing I'm committed to, it's running a squeaky clean business. Number one on my list of iron-clad rules?

Don't screw your customers.

But what's a guy to do when she's so hard to resist? How hard can it be to keep our hands off each other for a quick group tour down the hills and over the trails? I'm about to find out, and I have a feeling I'm going to need a new badge of honor because things are about to get **very hard in the woods.**

HARD WOOD

By Lauren Blakely

To be the first to find out when all of my upcoming books go live click here!

PRO TIP: Add lauren@laurenblakely.com to your contacts before signing up to make sure the emails go to your inbox!

Did you know this book is also available in audio and paperback on all major retailers? Go to my website for links!

PROLOGUE

By now, most women have met the half dozen or so basic types of men in the world.

Just to be sure, though, let's review the lineup.

First, there's the too-cool-for-school playboy who solemnly swears he'll never settle down. Next to him in the modern-day parade of dudes is the Grouchy McGrouch Pants. This surly, bearded guy is a softie beneath the dickhead exterior he shows to the world, along with his beanie cap. By his side is the guarded businessman in his three-piece suit, housing deep, dark secrets that only one woman can unlock. We have other roles in Guy Central Casting: the lumbersexual, the groomed father, the citified pretty boy, the hot nerd, and the bad boy with a heart of gold.

Trust me when I say the ladies of the world have heard every one of their stories.

I know that because I've fucking heard them. I've heard them from the guys, and I've heard them from the gals. When you take people out of their comfort zone and into the woods, they tend to tell you everything—every sordid detail. I'm honestly kind of amazed that men and women, women and women, and men and men get together at all. There's so much baggage going around, it's like a goddamn virus.

As for me?

I'm simple. I travel light. I don't bring luggage to the table. I hoist my backpack and I'm ready to go.

I'm a man of many skills. Give me a battery and I'll start a campfire. Show me an old phone and I'll make a compass. I'm the guy who knows how to get out of jams. I can fix a tire, repair a sink, gut a fish, pick a lock, and survive a bear attack—I've been there, done that, and have the merit badges to prove it.

Not gonna lie. Women do tend to like a guy who can get shit done without bitching about it. That's why I've had a nice run of luck with the ladies. But I'm not looking just to get lucky anymore.

I'm ready for a whole lot more.

I'd like to think that makes me the good guy with all the skills when we're talking about types. I'm the unicorn, and I'm not just talking about the length of my horn, if you catch my drift.

I'm the guy who's fit, successful, baggage-fucking-free, and—wait for it—ready to settle down.

Just call me a four-leaf clover.

The trouble is the woman I want is off-limits. She's my buddy's sister. But don't worry. That's not the issue. Max is a cool cat, and he has no problem with the fact that I have it bad for his little sis.

The problem is something else entirely, and I have one week to fix it. This is where all my life-hacking skills will have to come into play.

Let's do this.

1

Human beings tend to overthink all sorts of stuff, but a lot of our quandaries are pretty basic. You're either going out to dinner at the new Italian joint, or you're staying home to make a turkey sandwich. You're doing the laundry so you have a fresh shirt to wear, or you're sniffing the hamper, hunting for an old-but-good-enough-ie. You either carve out the time to run five miles, or you watch another ten episodes of *Breaking Bad*.

For the record, the answers are Italian, wash on hot, and lace up.

I take the same straightforward approach to the current black-and-white question posed to me by Camilla Montes, the local WRBC Channel 10 morning news anchor.

"Patrick, how will our viewers know if Fluffy wants to go for a hike?" she asks in that perfectly modulated TV reporter voice that matches her coiffed black hair.

"If you're wondering if Tiger, Tom, or Tabby is ready

to become an adventure cat, there's a simple litmus test any pet owner can conduct." I sit on the couch across from her and run a hand down Zeus's back. He arches into my palm and rumbles, his purr so loud he could land a career in the cat sound-effects business. *Show-off.* But in his defense, if I possessed an Al Green-style purr, I'd make sure the ladies heard it all the time, too. "I like to call it the drag or no-drag cat."

"Interesting. Tell us more," she says, her voice dripping with curiosity.

"Your cat either willingly lets you put a leash around his furry neck, or he turns into putty when you harness him, and you wind up dragging his feline butt across the floor." I mime tugging a gone-limp cat on a leash.

"That does make it crystal clear." Camilla flashes her practiced grin, then points a polished fingernail at me. "But how did you know to try with Zeus? Did you simply want a famous hiking partner, or did he insist on it?"

"I listened to the cat." I lean forward, parking one hand on my knee where my cargo shorts end, since the station likes me to dress like an REI model for my segments on *Tips and Tricks for Enjoying the Great Outdoors.* "His behavior told me he might be willing. For instance, one time, I headed down the hallway to drop the trash in the chute, and Zeus followed me out the door of the apartment, staying by my side the whole time." I lower my voice, cup the side of my mouth, and speak in a stage whisper. "And I don't think it was *only* because there was leftover salmon in the trash."

Camilla laughs.

"Salmon aside, he exhibited this inquisitive behavior often, and that's when I decided to give a leash and harness a whirl."

"And now he's become The Hiking Tomcat." She gestures grandly to my long-haired cat, who's lounging next to me, his white-gloved paws folded in front of his chest and a look of satisfaction on his furry face. I swear this dude is such a ham. He was born for the cameras. "Can you show our viewers how a cat who likes to go for hikes will handle being harnessed?"

"Why, I thought you'd never ask," I say as I stand, grab the leash and harness from the couch, and pat my leg.

Zeus stretches, slinks down the side of the couch, and gazes up at me.

"Want to go for a hike?"

His tail swishes back and forth.

Look, I'm not claiming he understands English. He's a cat, after all, not some kind of Cesar Milan-trained dog. But Zeus knows the drill, and the leash is dangling in my hand. He stretches his neck out, almost as if he's inviting me to put the red hiking harness over his head. I slide it on and clip his leash to the end. Zeus struts a few feet.

Camilla's smile beams as brightly as the TV lights blasting from above. "There you go."

"Would you like to walk him, Camilla?"

Her glossy red lips part in a wide grin. "I would love to walk this Internet superstar."

I place a finger to my lips. "Shh. We don't want his fame to go to his head."

"If he only knew how purr-fectly popular he is." Camilla takes the leash and walks Zeus around the set. "We brought in something to simulate the conditions on the trails."

Camilla escorts my boy to some fake rocks set up for this demo while the on-air screen shows an Internet video I've shot of Zeus clambering up a hill on a nearby trail. When they reach the rocks, the shot returns to Camilla, walking alongside in heels as Zeus scurries up the rocks and then down the other side. Note to self—score this cat some commercial work and see if we can retire on Friskies royalties.

But then, I've no interest in slowing down. My life is the textbook definition of *so fucking good*. My business is thriving, my family is healthy and happy, and my friends are settling down. There's only one thing I long for more of. Well, not a thing. More like a lovely, captivating, I-just-click-with-her *someone*.

But now's not the time to dwell on a certain woman.

Camilla returns to her blue chair, and I park myself on the couch again, alongside my loyal companion. I spend the next forty-five seconds reviewing trail safety for those who walk with their cats. After all, hiking with a feline is not for the faint of heart. People with dogs have no idea how easy they have it. Hiking with a feline is a whole other kettle of fish, but well worth it for the photos alone. We're talking unexpected goldmine. When my sister, Evie, plunked this cat on my doorstep and begged me to give him a home, I had no idea he'd turn out to be, one, totally cool, and two, the best marketing ever for my adventure tour company.

When the segment ends, Camilla thanks me and cuts to a commercial. "See you again next week, Patrick. I've been thinking we could do a piece on first aid in the woods."

"Absolutely."

"And you know what I've been dying to have you do a segment on?"

"Whatever you want, I can do it," I say, keeping up the easygoing vibe, since that's what works best for business partners.

"What if we did a piece on how to glamp?"

I chuckle lightly, rubbing a palm across my short, neat beard. "I can do that, and I can also give you a simple trick for camping with style right now if you'd like."

Her chocolate-brown eyes twinkle with excitement. "Please do."

"Do you have your phone with you?"

"Of course. It's on silent, but I'm never without my closest companion," she says, taking it from her skirt pocket, unlocking the screen, and handing it to me.

I tap a few words into the search bar, and the result I need returns quickly. I hand the phone to Camilla. "This is who you call."

Her reaction is priceless—a slow smile spreads as the name and number for the Ritz Carlton appears on her screen.

"So true. What can I say? I'm not an outdoorsy person at all. But I love your segments. So does my new intern, Taylor," she says, lowering her voice and looking toward a bubbly blonde who's waiting to escort me from the set. Funny, since my job requires me to find my way out of pretty much anywhere on God's great, green earth. Not to mention, I've been the guest commentator for the station's Friday morning outdoors segment for a few months now and I know the way to the door.

Then, because I like the furry dude and don't want to torture him—and taking a cat for a walk on the sidewalks of Manhattan is a unique and terrible form of torture—I drop Zeus into my backpack, slide the straps on, and leave the studio with the perky cheerleader by my side and the cat's silvery head poking out the top of the pack.

"I made s'mores the other day," Taylor offers with a big smile, her bright blue eyes meeting mine. "They were so good."

Her *so* has eight syllables and all of them drip with innuendo.

"That's great," I say, since I'm not interested in entertaining any syllables or innuendo with someone barely past puberty.

"Do you like s'mores, Patrick?"

"Who doesn't like s'mores?"

"I was wondering, though, if you might have any tips for me on how to make them. Like, how do I get the chocolate and marshmallow to *come* together perfectly?" She stops at the door, leans her hip against it suggestively, and twirls a strand of her hair.

And I do believe s'mores porn is officially a thing.

Even though I pride myself on making the world's greatest version of the campfire treat, I keep my answer simple, but clear. "It's all in how long you let the ingredients *age*," I say, since Taylor is twenty, twenty-one at best. "See you next week."

I say goodbye and leave, catching a train downtown then walking through the streets of lower Manhattan.

Do I get stares because of the cat on my back?

Hell, yeah.

Do I enjoy it?

Absolutely.

I smile and nod, giving a few salutes and a couple of *how are yous* and even a *meow* as a little kid walks by with her mom and whispers while pointing at my shoulder. As if I don't know there's a badass pussycat purring in my ear.

As I turn onto the block with my building, he's not the only one purring.

Because right there in front of the lobby, wearing reflective sunglasses and jeans that hug her curves deliciously, is a certain woman I'm very happy to see.

Mia Summers. Tiny but mighty. A powerful sprite with wavy hair, hazel eyes, a soft heart, and a quick wit I just dig.

I met her several months ago when she was visiting her brother, Max, and it's safe to say she's claimed center stage in my mind ever since.

When I see Mia, when I talk to Mia, when I spend time with Mia, it confirms my belief that some things are simple.

Like whether a cat drags his whole body on the floor or he gamely trots alongside you.

It's a yes or no.

A black or white.

You're either attracted to your good friend's sister or you're not.

For the record, the answer is I am, so fucking much.

2

I haven't seen Mia in almost a month, since the last time she was in town staying with Max. I didn't realize she'd be back a full week before her other brother Chase's wedding, and am I ever glad to see her again.

She makes all parts of me quite happy indeed.

By happy, I mean hard as a rock.

Okay, fine. It's not like I'm operating at full power this second. I'm thirty-three, not fifteen. I have plenty of self-control in the "when and where to pitch a tent" arena. All I'm saying is this woman gets me going, and I feel that zip down my body when I see her.

She's on the phone, her eyebrows pinched, her expression harried. She drags her hand through her caramel-blond hair. As I walk closer, I hear her say, "I understand. Yes, I understand. Things happen."

And that's the sound of someone being disappointed.

Which is a terrible thing for this sexy-as-a-fiery-sunset woman to experience.

When she stops and ends her call, she spots me. She tilts her head, her eyes piercing, her brow furrowed, and her dimples killing me with cuteness. Her eyes roam from me to Zeus, and then she points at my boy. "I don't know if anyone has told you this . . ."

I raise my eyebrows. "Tell me. What could it possibly be?"

Her eyes drift to the ground then back up. In a deadpan tone, she says, "But your shoelaces don't match."

I glance down at the red lace in my right hiking boot and the orange one in the left. "True that. The other red one got tangled on a tree trunk on the Hudson River Trail, and I had to sacrifice it to the shoelace gods."

"I'm sure they were delighted to receive such a fine offering," Mia says, and I love that even though I haven't seen her in a while, she rolls right into an easy conversation. No need for greetings, embraces, or *how the hell are yous*. Not that I'd object to her wrapping her arms around me and giving me a friendly hug. Or a long, lingering hug for that matter.

She's looking at me expectantly, and I snap back to our playful footwear banter. "They were indeed grateful that the shoelace came home to rest."

"Also," she says, stepping closer. "Did you know there's a cat in your hat? Well, on your back, actually."

"There is?" I crane my neck to peer over my shoulder. "You're right. How did he get there?"

She parks her hands on her hips. "You're in big trouble."

"I've been bad, have I?"

She pushes my shoulder then wags her finger at me. "How did you keep this from me?"

I quirk an eyebrow. "The fact that there's an awesome new Italian place down the street? It opened last month, and I planned to tell you."

She huffs, rolling her eyes. "I've known you for months and you didn't tell me you had a cat. Friends don't hide pets from friends."

She's not in town that often. She hasn't ever been to my apartment. And I don't take Zeus upstairs to Max's. But I'm not going to state the obvious. I'm going to have a little fun with her. Flirt with her. Because . . . that's what we do.

"There's a reason for that."

Her eyes go wide, and she taps her toe, waiting. I drag a hand through my hair. Evie says my light brown hair is floppy, and she tells me this is a good thing. *The ladies love floppy hair,* she says. She's been right so far. My hair's been a big hit with the ladies, and other parts have, too.

"It's a good reason," I add.

"I'm waiting, Patrick. This really isn't the type of intel you should hold back."

I heave a sigh as if I'm going to make a huge admission, then I park a hand on her shoulder. Because, well, I'm a sneaky bastard and I'll look for any opening to touch her. "Look, I'm going to be blunt. If I told you I had a hiking cat who rides shotgun in a backpack and can purr like he's a jazz superstar, you'd have had no choice but to fall in love with me." I flash her a grin.

When Mia laughs, she tips her head back and her wavy hair flutters in the breeze. She has a simple beauty about her. She's fresh-faced, and her hair isn't overly styled—it looks tousled and towel-dried, and I can't deny how much that wash-and-wear, low-maintenance vibe turns me on. Plus, she has the most fantastic dimples, which make her look innocent even though I suspect she has a wickedly naughty side. And then there are those eyes—hazel, with flecks of green. Sometimes they read as a soft, warm brown, sometimes like a green sea under the sun.

Don't even get me started on her body—toned and athletic, exactly what I like. But it's her dry sense of humor that nails me every time.

"How do you know I wouldn't have fallen in love with the cat instead?" She reaches up, standing on tiptoe since I'm nearly a foot taller than she is, and runs her hand down Zeus's head. Lady-killer that he is, Zeus lifts his chin and purrs suggestively as Mia scratches him.

And now we're at steel level.

Because with her this close, I can't help but enjoy the eyeful of soft, sweet curves at the line of her tank top. God, I love summer and the clothes women wear when the days turn warmer.

"Nah, we're a package deal," I say. "And look, don't be ashamed. You can just admit you want me now."

Mia steps back, rolls her eyes, and pushes her pink messenger bag higher on her shoulder.

I gesture to the lobby so we can head inside. Her beauty products company is based in San Francisco, but she's been spending more and more time in New York. When she's in town, she usually crashes at Max's apartment, five floors up from mine. I first met Max when I moved into this building a year and a half ago, and we became fast friends. But I didn't meet Mia until she started travelling to New York regularly for business several months ago.

She holds up her hands in surrender. "Fine, fine. He's pretty much sealed the deal for me." Her eyelids flutter, and she places her hand on her heart, making a loud thumping sound. "I'm over the moon."

"Exactly. That's why I didn't just whip out my cat and show him to you the first night we met. Or the second. Zeus is a complete and absolute lady magnet, and since I respect you, I couldn't willy-nilly throw down this kind of secret weapon and leave you no choice."

"Zeus is kind of a big, bold name. Is that overcompensation for something?" Her eyes drift down. Thank fuck I'm not sporting wood anymore.

I scoff. "Overcompensation for his sheer and utter awesomeness."

"And what makes him so awesome? Besides the fact that he rides sidecar with you, it seems."

We reach the elevator banks, and I stab the up button. "You can play it cool, but I'm sure you've heard of Zeus The Hiking Tomcat. He has more than a million followers on Instagram."

She blinks, and the sarcasm games cease. "Seriously?"

As we wait, I snag my phone and open The Hiking

Tomcat's feed, showing her some recent pictures: a shot of the furry fellow wandering along a curved mountain trail, a picture of him chilling in the stern of a canoe as I paddle across a lake, an image of him scurrying on a felled tree trunk over a mountain stream.

Then, my favorite—Zeus in the meadow, his eyes closed, his face raised to the sun, enjoying some rays at the top of a four-mile hike up a mountain when there was nothing but blue skies forever.

"Wow. I can't believe he actually hikes," she says.

"I can take you along, if you want to see the proof with your own eyes."

She laughs and shakes her head, patting her bag. "I just arrived last night. I have meetings all afternoon, terms with suppliers to review, and marketing campaigns to peruse. Plus, dinner tomorrow night with Josie and Chase, and Max and Henley. I have way too much work to take a break for a hike."

The elevator arrives. We step inside and the doors whoosh shut.

"There's always time for a hike."

She sighs heavily, so hard it's like air leaks out of her. "I feel like I don't even have time to breathe, let alone go to the gym, let alone go on a trip. The last time I was in town, I barely made it to the Friday afternoon laser tag game with my friend Dylan. And I just found out one of our biggest suppliers has pulled out of a deal for this new face wash we've been working on," she says, meeting my gaze. "And I need to figure out a replacement."

Mia started her own company a few years ago,

making organic and cruelty-free beauty products and makeup. It's a true passion of hers, and she works doggedly at building up Pure Beauty. But even when you love what you do, it can exact a toll. I see a flash of weariness in her eyes, tiredness, and I sense how much this woman needs a break.

"That's what I was doing before I saw you. Talking to the supplier," she explains.

Ah, so I was right. Disappointed. "Sorry, Mia. That sucks."

"I know. I'm trying so hard, and I just feel like I'm being pulled in all these directions."

"Maybe you do need to get away."

"I can't."

"You'll think better after a few hours unplugged. Be in a better mood for the wedding next week." Look, I'm not simply trying to snag some extra time with the woman. I can tell from the tightness in her shoulders, the heaviness of her sigh, and, oh yeah, her mother-fucking words that Mia needs a break, even a short one.

"Is that so?"

"Mia, you need to recharge. Look, I'm sure you can fill all twenty-five hours in your day with work, but people need to step back from the screens, too."

"Except there are only twenty-four hours in a day, right?"

The elevator slows at my floor. When the door opens, I stand in it to keep talking to her. "Not for people like you, who have somehow annexed an extra hour to squeeze in even more productivity. So take a break for a couple of hours and let yourself unwind. Your mind will be fresher."

She nibbles on the corner of her lips. "You're trying to get me to play hooky."

"Tomorrow is Saturday. If not working all day long on a Saturday counts as playing hooky, we have some serious issues."

"What are you suggesting we do?"

"I'm saying we find some sunshine and snacks, and unplug till you clear your head and let go of this stress."

The gold flecks in her eyes twinkle, making them look green. "I do like snacks."

"Marcona almonds," I say in a low, dirty whisper.

She hums.

"Green olives." My voice turns huskier.

She fans herself.

"Sunflower seeds."

She lets out a gasp, and yeah, sunflower seed erotica is way better than s'mores smut. "Now you're just teasing me."

"I swear. All those can be yours."

"But I have to review these marketing campaigns . . ."

The elevator rumbles, itching to travel to the next floor. I make my last pitch. "I wonder if there are any tall, handsome, blue-eyed, brilliant fellow business owners who'd look at them with you, say, over lunch today, so that tomorrow you could take a day off to relax."

I see her switch from maybe to yes. I suspect it was the word *lunch*.

She bounces on her toes. "Can we order Italian from that new place down the street?"

And lunch is now my wingman.

"Deal," I say, and she follows me off the elevator and into my spacious apartment. I set down my pack, letting Zeus go free. He hops out, and once his white paws hit the floor, he promptly proceeds to bestow all the affection in the world on Mia's leg.

We spend the next two hours eating pasta primavera, reviewing her marketing campaigns, and debating favorite foods to bring along on a four-hour hike.

We settle on the aforementioned olives and almonds, and then she places an order of *surprise me since I love surprises*.

When she leaves, I batten down the hatches and take care of my own business, coordinating with my new West Coast manager who oversees our Northern California trips, as well as my associates out here who handle day-to-day work on the hiking, rafting, camping, and corporate retreats we manage on this coast. In the afternoon, my HR manager calls, and we spend an hour reviewing the updated employee handbook line by line. I had some trouble earlier this year with a guide who slept with a married client on a three-day hiking trip in Vermont. The whole situation turned into a mess—the guide slapped some angry posts on Facebook about being fired, and the client's husband called and threatened us. Tempers flared red-hot and dangerous, even though nothing came of it at the end of the day. But we tightened our guidelines for employees, since that's all we can control anyway.

* * *

The next morning I'm up bright and early for a five-mile run, and when I return, I slide the red harness onto Zeus. I snap a shot of him sitting next to a daypack and some food for the hike, then post it to his feed.

Ready for today's adventure!

I shake my head because I can't believe this is who I've become. A guy who posts cell phone pics of his cat.

But, then again, how could I turn him down when Evie brought him to me, his green eyes batting up at me like Puss in Boots? My sister is a matchmaker, and one of her clients is a fireman. He rescued Zeus from a warehouse fire in Queens. The little fellow had no home, so Evie insisted he be mine, since she's mildly allergic.

Ergo, I have a cat.

A few minutes later, I take the elevator to Max's floor and knock on his door.

He answers and bestows the biggest scowl on earth on me. "Did you think I wouldn't notice you were taking my sister out for the day?"

I roll my eyes at Max's effort to play the role of scary big brother. Even though we've known each other for less than two years, he's become my closest friend in New York, in part because he's blunt, loyal, dependable, and has a kickass pool table. *His* opinion always matters to me.

"I figured showing up at your door would tip you off."

But he doesn't ease up. Instead, he snarls.

That only makes me laugh. "Dude, the whole routine is a little ridiculous."

"I saw the way you looked at her at Henley's dinner party a few weeks ago."

Max and his girlfriend, Henley, built a car together for a network TV show that just finished a successful first season, and they celebrated with a party at their place. Not gonna lie—I spent a little extra time with Mia at the party, but I hadn't seen her in a while, and the two of us always seem to gravitate toward each other when she's in town. We've been like that from the night we met—we click.

And that's a big reason why it sucks that she lives three thousand miles away.

But since Max started it, I can't resist giving him a hard time. "And at this party, how exactly did I look at her? Like I wanted to help serve the salad she made? That kind of look?" I adopt a low and dirty voice just to emphasize the ridiculousness of his point. "Hey there, sweet cheeks. Let me help you with the tongs."

"Don't ever let me hear you say the words 'sweet cheeks' again."

"Same goes for you."

He cracks a smile, laughs loudly, and smacks me on the back. "Just yanking your chain. I know you'd never do anything behind my back."

Well, that's not entirely true. I did some seriously dirty things to her in my imagination this morning.

"Right?" he asks, pressing.

I raise my hand, as if I'm taking an oath. "Nothing behind your back, I promise. Besides, when I convince your sister to marry me, I'll be upfront about it. Man to man." I smack his chest.

He blinks. Rubs his ear. "You're messing with me."

I smirk, my lips twitching in an evil grin. "Absolutely," I say, since there's nothing to tell. I meant what I said—I *would* be upfront about it. I *would* tell him. But there's nothing to tell, because she lives so far away. All I can do is grab the few seconds and minutes of time with her that I can. Maybe if I spend enough hours with Mia, the feeling will burn off and fade away. "Besides," I add, "I'm just taking her to explore Mother Nature. I have the sense she needs it."

"Man, she does," Max says, peering behind him. "She's been stressed about the business, where it's going, what to do next. Henley and I tried to convince her to get a massage, but then she mentioned she was spending the day with you. I was glad to hear it."

"Good. I guess that means you'll let me borrow your Triumph to take her to the trailhead."

Max sets a hand on his stomach and laughs. "That's a good one. As if I'd let anyone but my woman touch Blue Betty. You can take your Hyundai."

A few minutes later, Mia appears, twisting her damp hair into a bun on top of her head and flashing me a smile. "I'm ready. I have to be back by five thirty for a conference call with a potential supplier. She had some time today so we're going to chat."

I roll my eyes and whisper to Max, "Someone needs to cancel that Saturday conference call."

Mia parks her hands on her hips. "I heard you. This apartment is big, but not that big."

"Don't forget dinner tonight with your favorite brother," Max says drily, tapping his chest.

"You mean Chase?" Mia asks, batting her eyes innocently.

He scowls. "Fine, I'll let him come along." His tone turns serious. "Henley said to remind you we have reservations for seven thirty, and Chase and Josie are excited to see you."

"I'll be back. I swear. You act like I'm going to get stuck in the woods."

Max scoffs. "No. I'm not worried about that at all. I'm worried you're going to get stuck on your conference call."

A few minutes later, Mia slides into my most-decidedly-not-a-Hyundai Jeep, and as we make our way out of Manhattan, she pets Zeus, who's decided to spend the drive on her lap.

Can't say I blame him.

I wouldn't mind spending some time there, too.

3

───────

I have a rule of thumb if I like a woman.

Call me old-fashioned.

But here's what I do.

I ask her on a date.

I know, I know. I'm old-school, especially since I use the phone to do it.

I don't send coy texts. I don't Snapchat her a *Wassup?* And I don't try to weasel a hookup. I call her and invite her out. I try to choose an activity that suits her. For the athletic ones, I might suggest a bike ride. For the casual gals, maybe an afternoon at a craft beer festival. For the Louboutin-styled lady, I find sushi or the latest hip eatery that fits the bill. There's no need to half-ass anything in life, especially a first date. I go all out and make sure we can truly get to know each other. Find out if we're compatible.

I haven't asked Mia out, though, and it's not because of Max. Not really. The guy is a total softie inside. Plus, he's not, ya know, a dickhead who'd pull that whole *don't date my sister because she's my sister* bullshit.

The bigger reason is she's not around that much. I suppose I'm not, either. But she's *really* not around. She doesn't even live here. She lives in San Francisco, and though she makes it to New York enough for me to have developed a wicked attraction to her that shows no signs of abating, she's not here enough for me to realistically pursue dating her. Or mating her. Or more.

We pull up at a trail near the town of Cold Spring in the Hudson Valley, and I try to shove all thoughts of attraction out of my head. That involves some seriously intense mental gymnastics, since Mia is completely fetching in her khaki shorts, white sneakers, and a sky-blue scoop-neck shirt. When she unzips the light hoodie that she's been wearing, I read her T-shirt. It says "I'm sorry for what I said when I was hungry."

After I harness up Zeus, I nod at her shirt and say, "Good thing I packed two servings of surprise food for you. I take it this means you're one of those people for whom *hangry* is a real word?"

She narrows her eyes at me. "You know how some people are before coffee?"

I nod.

"That's me unfed."

I laugh as we head for the trailhead, enjoying the sun shining brightly above. "We need a food mood ring for you. It would detect your probable mood based on what fuel you've consumed, and it would warn me when stores are dangerously low."

"I had oatmeal and blueberries this morning, so the arrow should still point in the *pleasant* range, but in a few hours, it'll drop precipitously into *disagreeable*."

"Good thing I'm prepared."

Mia makes eye contact with my backpack. "Looks like you're prepared for everything."

I know too well the risks of getting lost in the woods, so I've packed some of the basics. Better to be safe than sorry. "I am."

I gesture to the soft dirt path that unfurls ahead of us at the base of the hill before it winds into a more wooded section. "After you."

She holds up her hand as a stop sign, then points at me, accusatorially. "Wait. Aren't you supposed to be the nature guide?"

I run a hand through my hair. "Yes, but the way I see it is if I send you ahead, you'll be my canary so I'm aware of any jagged rocks, quicksand, snakes, mountain lions, or even the occasional man-eating twig."

She shoots me a steely stare. "If the twigs are man-eaters, then they'll be aiming for you." She spins around and takes off in a sprint, initiating a full-on, all-out, shotgun-has-fired race. "Catch me if you can!"

Holy shit.

She's a blur.

She glances over her shoulder, waving to egg me on.

I'm fast, too. I could catch up in seconds. The trouble is, Zeus is allergic to running. Sure, he can tear off in hot pursuit of a small, and likely, tasty bird. But that's about the extent of his speed footwork. He's not playing Mia's game. Instead, he puts one white paw in front of the other and walks.

And walks.

And walks.

"Dude, you're cock-blocking me," I mutter to the cat.

He lifts his face and utters an *au contraire* meow.

"Can you try to at least jog?"

If cats could laugh, Zeus would be doubled over as he strolls after the woman.

"How about a trot? Maybe a power walk?"

A minute later, I've caught up to Mia, who's laughing, her hands on her hips. "I'll take my medal now, please."

"And what event is that in?"

"In leaving you in the dust," she says, shaking her hips back and forth, like a badass trash-talker. I see taking Mia out of the city has made her even feistier.

"I had a handicap. My cat."

"Aww. Poor Zeus." She bends to scratch his ears. He stretches up into her palm. "I'm sorry Patrick is blaming you for him being slow."

I roll my eyes, shaking my head in amusement. "One, I'm not slow. But two, you're a jackrabbit."

She rises. "Not a cheetah?"

"Anyone can call you a cheetah. Not everyone knows jackrabbits are the seventh fastest land animal. However," I say, gesturing to the gray boy by my side, "the humble house cat is not on the list at all. Hence, we stroll today."

She shrugs and smiles, a grin full of mischief, as we begin our trek. "'I took a walk in the woods and came out taller than the trees.'"

She's quoting Thoreau. She's not helping things at all. I was a lit major in college, and his work inspired me. His writings on nature were my drug. Nope, there's very little Mia can do, it seems, to make me not want her.

"That's a good one. But my favorite of his is, 'If one advances confidently in the direction of his dreams, and endeavors to live the life which he has imagined, he will meet with a success unexpected in common hours.'"

"I love that. I even love the simplified version you see in those inspirational quotes."

"Live the life you've imagined," I begin, and she jumps in to finish with me. "Go confidently in the direction of your dreams."

I smile, impressed.

Her smile spreads, too, shifting from playfulness to warmth. "There's a shop at SFO Airport that has magnets with all sorts of popular business and life quotes. You know—dream big, work hard, innovate, pivot. I always stop to read them, since they give me a warm glow. But I love that one best. Because I want that life." She glances at the cat. "Speaking of dreams, it's one of mine to say I walked a cat. May I?"

I hand her the leash, and she beams. Just fucking beams. And that smile hooks into me, lighting me up, so I step closer, lower my voice, and say, "The reason I said 'after you' at the start of the trail is that I'm a gentleman, and I still believe that ladies come first." I stop, reining in a smirk. "Go first, I mean. Ladies go first."

Her pupils dilate, and she blinks. Then, her shoulders rise and fall, more dramatically than before. Good. If she's going to beguile me with quotes from my favorite philosopher–poet, then perhaps I'll tease her with a little wordplay, too. Of the dirtier variety. The kind that'll make her imagine. Make her feel. Make her wonder.

"That's considerate of you. And I do like gentlemen," she says, a slight catch in her breath when she says *like.*

Maybe if she weren't flying home in mere days, I'd follow that with a flirty reply. I'd test the waters, ask what she meant, and if all signs pointed to go, I'd act on it. After all, this is a perfect setting for a kiss. The sun is rising overhead. The sky is a paint can of blue. A canopy of trees frames Mia.

Sunshine, lip gloss, and her. That's what I'd taste if I pressed my mouth to hers the way I want.

But she's given no indication she wants a kiss.

I step around her on the path, pointing to a gnarly twig for her to avoid.

"Man-eating variety?" she asks as we walk.

"That one likes speedy women, so be careful."

"Thanks for the warning. And since you were right about twigs, does that mean you were accurate about snakes on this trail?"

Her voice is calm and even, unlike the way most

people talk about snakes. Usually the word comes out in a chilled whisper.

"There are some, sure. We're outdoors. But you don't see them too often, and I know how to handle them, so you don't have to worry." I study her face, looking for signs of fear. I don't see any. "You're not afraid of snakes, are you?"

"Let's put it this way—I'm not about to curl up on the couch and share popcorn with one, but I can deal with them."

Something furry, not reptilian, rustles in a bush ahead, and Zeus goes bananas. He lunges, jerking Mia with him, yanking her as he charges after his favorite thing in the world. The one thing he'll run after forever —a squirrel.

"His greatest dream is to have squirrel for a meal," I say as Mia gently tugs him away.

"Let me guess. He hasn't yet achieved that?"

I shake my head. "Not yet. But hope springs eternal." I cycle back to the conversation. "So, snakes don't scare you off. What are you afraid of?"

Her answer is immediate. "Balconies," she says, shuddering.

I arch a brow. "Balconies, as in decks?"

She nods vigorously.

"I'd never have guessed. Max's apartment is on the twenty-fifth floor."

She raises a finger as she sidesteps a low branch. "Aha. Therein lies the issue. I'm not afraid of being up high. I'm afraid of standing on a balcony."

Awareness dawns on me. "You either have the fear

of the balcony crumbling under you, or the one where you'll fling yourself off."

"The second one. It's so weird, isn't it?" she says, her voice full of seeming surprise that she feels this way. As if she doesn't entirely know what to make of this fear of hers. "I know logically I won't. I love life, and I don't have suicidal tendencies. But when I'm on a balcony, I'm supremely aware that I could hoist my leg over and jump off. It's such a strange fear, Patrick."

Her tone is intense, but what strikes me the most is the way she says my name. As if there's a special intimacy to this confession.

"I've never admitted that to anyone," she says, under her breath, almost astonished she gave this fear voice.

I'm pleased—proud, if I'm honest—she chose me for this confidence, but curious as to her reasoning. "Why haven't you told anyone?"

"Most people wouldn't understand it," she says, as a monarch butterfly flutters past my head, flapping its sun-yellow wings. I point to it as she talks, and she smiles, watching it fly away before she goes on. "Most people would worry it means I'm going to launch myself overboard, but that's not it. It's just that my brain can see all the horrible things unfolding. Even though I know rationally that I won't do them, the mind still lets the images unfurl. And that's how I feel when I stand on a balcony and look down. I *feel* all the things that could happen, and some ancient human curiosity pokes and prods at me, saying *test it out*, even though of course I don't want to."

"So why'd you tell me?"

Her eyes are a darker green than I've ever seen before as she answers. "You're different. You're not like everyone else."

And that's one of those things people say that can rock your world or upend it.

4

———

Different.

It's one of those adjectives that can go either way.

He's a little, how shall we say, different.

I've never thought of myself as different. I'm a regular guy. I'm not someone who has odd habits, like swabbing my ears with Q-tips in public, or discussing Q-tip swabbing in mixed company, for that matter, or even standing so close to strangers that they can smell my breath. Though, to be clear, it's minty fresh since I brush as if it's a religion.

But aside from walking a cat, I'm as regular as they come.

"Lay it on me, Mia. Tell me why you think I'm *different*. You don't like the beard?" I run my hand over my chin.

She laughs. "The beard is great."

"Clearly, you have something against dudes who like cats, then."

"Oh my God. I love animals. You know that. I volunteer at WildCare, helping injured wildlife. I do what I do because I love animals more than people most of the time."

"Then obviously, you found my high school yearbook photo."

She arches a brow, her eyes twinkling with curiosity. "No, but now I want to."

"Don't. Just don't," I say, my voice deeper, warning her. Because that right there is a line no one should cross.

"Fine, fine. I'll stop rifling through your underwear drawer for your yearbook."

Mia and my boxer briefs. I'm just going to linger on that thought for another second. Okay, back to the matter at hand.

"So I'm *different*?" I draw air quotes. "What's the story?"

She smiles broadly at me. "It's a compliment. You're different because you're normal."

A laugh starts deep in my belly, rumbles up my chest, and bursts from me. A hearty, happy laugh. "Normal. I'll take that."

"Trust me. It's a *huge* compliment. Most people aren't as easygoing as you. As laid-back. As *comfortable* with who they are. I think that's why I told you about the war I've been waging with balconies."

"I'm glad you shared your balcony battles."

She sighs deeply, as if she's inhaling the fresh, invigorating air. She stretches her neck from side to side and shimmies her shoulders, almost as if a weight has lifted. "You were right. Getting away from work and phones and pressure does help."

I flash her a smile, giving myself a mental fist bump. It makes me happy to know I've helped her.

She points to the trail. "Keep on going. It's your turn now. Tell your friend Mia—what are you afraid of, Patrick?"

"Vegas," I say, shuddering. "Can't stand that city."

"Oh, stop it. You're not afraid of Vegas."

"Fine. I just dislike it."

She laughs. "I like Vegas. It's fun. A little over-the-top, but I take it all in stride. Why do you hate it? You live in one of the biggest cities in the world."

"I don't really hate Vegas. But there's no balance to it like there is in New York City. See, Manhattan operates at a million miles an hour, but then it surprises you with Central Park and Hudson River Greenway, and then a cobblestoned street in the Village. And water—everywhere there's water."

She sighs happily. "I do love Manhattan, too. But you still haven't told me. Fears. Fess up. Be truthful."

So we're playing the getting-to-know-you game. I can do this. I like this. I want this. Plus, the answer is easy. My big fear? I've conquered it. I adjust my pack slightly, dropping my shades to my eyes since the sun is rising higher and hitting harder. "Bridges."

"Huh. That surprises me."

"Yeah?"

"I can't see that at all. Do you mean like a glass bridge with a view from one thousand feet above roaring waters? Or do you mean the rickety bridges in a jungle?"

"Rickety bridges I can handle. Even glass bridges. My issue was with the ones I have to drive over." It's my turn to shudder. "Those were mildly horrifying."

"Ohhhhh," she says, dragging out the word. "You're afraid of crashing, tumbling over the side of the bridge, and being stuck in a car."

I mime hammering. "Nailed it. But I got over it."

"How did you get over it? Did you buy a car with manual windows so you could always escape and swim free?"

"That, and I drive wearing flippers and goggles so I'm ready."

"Ha ha," she says, shoving my shoulder. "Seriously. What did you do? Because you were completely fine when we drove across that bridge over the Hudson."

"I kept doing it," I say, matter-of-factly. "I kept facing the fear. Stared it down, so to speak. Honestly, it was the hardest thing for me when I moved to Manhattan. So many bridges, right?"

"Like they've mated and produced baby bridges everywhere."

"Exactly. I had to deal with all the bridges. I played music to keep me in an upbeat zone, and actually talked back to myself as I drove over them. I said things like *I'm fine, I'm in control, I'm safe.*"

She smiles. "That's kind of cool. You took charge of your fear. You didn't let it control you. Is it gone entirely? Did you even think about it when we drove here?"

"Sure, it occurred to me. But I can handle it now." I take a beat, casting my gaze behind me to meet her eyes. I wink. "Though, next time it would be so much easier if you'd hold my hand."

"Want me to pet your hair and sing lullabies, too?"

"Yeah, maybe not."

"Okay, next order of business," she says as we wind along the trail, heading higher into the hills. "Tell me something you're still afraid of. Tell me a fear you haven't conquered, because otherwise I'll think you're not normal."

I scratch my chin, considering her question, as Zeus sniffs a purple wildflower tucked beside a small boulder. In the distance, I can make out the faint gurgling of a stream. The sound of water rippling over smooth stones is music to me. It means I'm outdoors. I'm moving. My legs are working. My heart is pumping blood. This is what I love. Energy. Action. *Living.* The way I feel under the big sky, with no pavement between the earth and my feet, is why I have one big fear.

"Here's one I don't think I'll ever get over," I say, raising my shades and leveling my gaze at her. No joking. No teasing. No sarcasm. "Being sick."

Her expression softens. Her lips part. She swallows. "I can see that about you."

"I want to be healthy. I want to be well. I want to make my own choices every day. Health is such a gift, and what I'm afraid of most is losing it for God knows what reasons."

"Like something catastrophic?"

"No, but yes. But it's also just anything—flu, cold,

whatever. I hate being sick. I don't ever want to be the unwell guy."

She brings her hand to her chest. "You're making me want to give you a hug."

Well, that is an unexpected bonus.

"I won't turn you down," I say playfully.

She steps closer, stands on tiptoe, and wraps her arms around me. She tucks her head against my pecs, her cheek on my shoulder. Oh hell. She fits me like the perfect pair of hiking boots. The kind that feel so good you want to spend your day in them. Her hair smells like pineapple. There's also a hint of coconut, and I know it's one of the products she makes—tropical body wash. I'd like to lick her neck, suck on her jaw, flick my tongue against her ear. I bet she'd shiver if I pressed my mouth to her. I bet she'd tremble if I nipped on that soft earlobe, then she'd arch into me, asking for more.

Begging for more.

But my dirty thoughts are washed clean instantly when she whispers into my shoulder. "I'm afraid of hurting my family."

"Yeah?" I ask, and all my instincts tell me to raise a hand and pet her hair. So I listen to my gut. I run a hand down her blond locks. Jesus. She's like a kitten. Her hair is so soft.

"I love my stupid brothers, and I want to do right by them. They always looked out for me when I was younger. I was the smallest kid in school."

"You were?"

She nods against my chest. "Shockingly, I didn't have the massive growth spurt all the way to five-foot-one until I turned fourteen. When I was in grade school, other kids teased me, saying I looked like I was still in nursery school. Even in second grade, the running joke was that I was a kindergartner. I hated it because I just wanted to fit in. And my brothers, they taught me it didn't matter. They taught me to be tough. They never made fun of me for my size. They did the opposite, in fact. Max was the one who said my size would come in handy for gymnastics. That it would be my secret weapon," she says, pulling back and meeting my eyes with an intense stare.

"He was? Our big, boorish Max?" I laugh, because that's kind of cool. Correction—that's incredibly cool.

The corner of her lips curve up. "Yep. Our big, boorish Max. He told me it was the one sport where being tiny would be a true advantage."

"He was right."

"My parents were totally supportive, too, but it was Max who was always there for me. He would get so excited when I'd win a competition. He'd cheer the loudest, lift me up on his shoulders when I won a gold. He was five years older, and when I was ten, he was already more than a foot taller than me. His enthusiasm was like an explosion of happiness in my chest," she says, tapping her breastbone. "And he was right. My focus on gymnastics made me stop caring that kids mocked me for being small."

"I like your size." Because really, what else is there to say? She's little, and it's perfect for her.

Her voice goes soft, kind of sexy. "I like yours."

And right now, I want to make s'mores porn with

her. I want to tug her back into my arms and show her how well our sizes fit.

But right when we're veering into the flirty, let's-compliment-each-other phase of getting-to-know-you, the sound of crunching footsteps ahead interrupts us.

A pair of hikers appears, heading in our direction as they go down the hill. That's my cue to move on from whatever moment we're having. We soldier on in silence, nearing a heavyset guy in safari shorts and a straw hat. The woman right behind him wears a small backpack and uses a walking stick.

I tip my forehead to them. "How are you doing?"

"Can't complain. It's a perfect day," the guy says.

"It sure is."

"And that's one helluva cat you have with you."

"Why, thank you," Mia chimes in as we step out of the way, letting them pass. "He's an adventure cat."

"Fred, why don't we train our Siamese to wear a harness?" the woman asks.

"Sweetheart, we have a no-drag cat. That's what I heard on TV yesterday."

Mia chuckles to herself. As she does, I flash back to their words. Not the ones about the cat. The ones before. *It's a perfect day.* That's a bold statement. I'm not so sure my day is perfect, but I'd have to say it's pretty damn good.

And, moment or no moment, that has to be enough. This is all I'll have with Mia – little moments every now and again.

* * *

A little later, we reach the water. The stream races downhill, rushing over rocks, cutting over stones. A huge tree trunk rests over the creek, providing passage to another trail.

Mia hands me the leash. "Watch me."

Easiest command ever.

She steps onto the log, crosses it as if it's a balance beam, dipping her foot along the side with each step, sticking out her chest, and flinging her arms up triumphantly. My heart skitters faster, and I can't help but worry about her, no matter how many gymnastics meets she won as a young girl. When she reaches the middle, she bends forward, sets her hands flat on the log, and kicks her legs straight up.

She's ruler straight, and beautiful upside down. Her hair spills to the wood, and she beams the wildest grin at me. "Like my handstand?"

"Love it, but please don't do a back handspring or whatever they're called," I warn, because I'm feeling like what she described feeling on a balcony—only I'm imagining Mia tumbling off the log.

"I didn't win the all-around fifth-grade gold for nothing." She flips over, nailing the landing. She leans forward now, her arms straight out to the side, one leg kicked high behind her. "Hey, Mr. Hooky! What do you think? Am I enjoying my day off?"

"Too much." I shake my head, laughing as I scoop up Zeus, drop him in the pack, and carry him across the log on my back. I keep him there as we climb a series of steep switchbacks to the top of a hill, where a meadow awaits.

"Wow," Mia says, her eyes roaming across the grass and flowers, admiring the view.

I'm admiring the view, too. Mia, standing in one of my favorite places on Earth. Maybe this *is* a perfect day.

I tap my watch. "Did we make it in time? Is the food mood ring pointing to *disagreeable*?"

Mia rubs her belly. "We're *this* close."

As I spread out a blanket, I'm struck by the thought that if this were someone else's story, she'd have tumbled on the log, I'd have caught her, played the hero, and we'd have shared a moment. But our moment came before she flipped upside down on a felled tree. Our moment transpired on the trail when she hugged me out of the blue, and for several fantastic seconds I had a taste of how well we'd fit.

As I unpack the food, I wonder if we'll experience any more moments, or if today is all I have before I have to get serious about letting go of this crush once and for all.

5

———————

Mia groans. "I'm stuffed."

"How is that possible?" I lean back on the red-checked blanket spread out on the grass. "You barely ate anything."

"Not true. For the record, I devoured the surprise strawberries, the almonds, the Gouda cheese, the yummy crackers, and the olives. Everything but the turkey jerky."

"You do realize you just rattled off snacks. That's all you ate. Snacks. Not a meal."

"Now you have something against snack food. Are you a snack-ist?"

"Quite the opposite. I happen to think snacks are among the greatest joys in life."

She rests on her elbows, her legs stretched in front of her, crossed at the ankles, and turns her gaze to me. "And what are the others?"

I meet her eyes straight on. "Sex."

Her expression is blank at first, then a laugh bursts from her lips. "Well, yeah. But what else?"

My eyes bug out. "That's not enough for you?"

"You said 'joys,' as in plural. I was waiting to hear the others."

"Ah, simple misunderstanding," I say, nodding. "See, the answer was plural because with me, the sex is so good it's multiplied." Then I wiggle my eyebrows.

Once more her face is a tabula rasa, and then her entire body shudders. We're talking head-to-toe laughter. "You sound like the dirty kangaroo meme now. You know him?"

"Oddly enough, I'm not familiar with the filthy marsupial."

"He's a douchey marsupial," she corrects. "Anyway, he's this weirdly muscular kangaroo, lying down, looking like a '70s porn star, all suave and cocky as he says things like, 'Hey girl, ever been down under?'"

I scratch my chin. "So what you're saying is I'm a douchey kangaroo, and you don't like sex multiplied. Fair enough."

She fixes me with a *you've got to be kidding* stare as she sits up to swat my elbow. "That was for saying something ridiculous. Obviously, I like multiplication. It's my favorite form of arithmetic," she says, giving me a very naughty wink that sets off a new round of lust in me, as I picture how she'd look after two times two orgasms.

The answer? That's what a perfect day looks like.

Flopping back down, she takes a deep breath and raises her face to the sky as if she's soaking in the sun's rays. She sticks out her flat belly and adds to the look by ballooning her cheeks. "But maybe no plurals or multiplication for me when I have a snack baby growing."

I raise an eyebrow. Her belly is a board. A sensual, alluring board I want to kiss all over. Yeah, that's what Mia does to me. Gets me aroused thinking of kissing her board belly. "You can't even make your belly look full."

"Yes, I can," she says, huffing and puffing and trying hard to make her midsection round. "Just feel it. You can feel the snacks growing inside me."

I stretch an arm across to pat her tight, trim belly, wishing for a second I was feeling it under different circumstances. But even I'm not enough of a pervert to be turned on by her pretend belly. Her goofball side? That's another matter entirely. It's endearing and, admittedly, enticing.

I wish it weren't.

"Do you have a turkey jerky baby in you?" she asks, her tone intensely serious.

I pat my abs. "Definitely."

"Do you think Zeus has a tuna baby in his furry belly?"

"Absolutely," I say, glancing at Zeus, lolling in a tuna coma. I pick up the empty can of fish from his side and place it in the trash bag.

"Anyway," Mia begins, her tone shifting, "can I be serious for a moment?"

I point my thumb over my shoulder as if gesturing to the past. "You weren't serious just then?"

"Ha ha. But what I wanted to say is thank you. I was a stress case about work, and even though I didn't work today, the time I spent here cleared my mind. I feel like I can go back and tackle the problems. And while we were hiking, I came up with several possibilities for new suppliers based in the area."

That piece of intel pricks my ears. "Think you'll be spending more time in New York, then?"

An *I wish* laugh falls from her lips. "Most of my work on the deals can be done remotely. Give me a screen, and I'm good to go. But I'm grateful you encouraged me to play hooky today. I needed it, and I can only imagine how beneficial this is for when you lead corporate groups. They must get so much out of it."

"I'd like to think they do. After the trust falls, of course."

She presses her hands together in prayer. "Please tell me you don't do trust falls."

"Any guide who works for my company signs two agreements—don't sleep with the customers, and never ever do a trust fall."

"You do need to have standards."

"And thank you, Mia," I say, stripping the teasing from my voice as the sun shines high above us now, warming my skin, bathing us in its afternoon glow. I'm fortunate that my corporate retreat business has grown in the last few years. A lot of companies use us for day trips for their employees, for rafting expeditions, and for weekend canoeing retreats. It's kind of cool to watch employees come together. "The reports back from that side of the business have been great. They say the trips foster bonding, improve morale, and help the employees adjust better to changes in their companies. I don't mean to sound like a broken record, but I think sometimes we forget that our bodies were designed to be active. We think best when we walk, or run, or stretch, or bend."

Mia flashes me a big smile that shows off her dimples, those adorable dimples that nail me in the heart every single time I see them. "I love that you've turned your passion into this huge success."

"Well, Zeus helped," I say, giving credit where it's due.

Mia sits up, stretching to pet him as he basks in the sun. "I feel like he has the right idea. Can we take a catnap?" As if to emphasize her point, her mouth opens into the hugest yawn I've ever seen.

"Catnaps are always a good idea. I only have one rule. We need to nap in a tent."

"You have a tent?"

I blink. "Sorry, what did you say? Do I have a tent? Do takeout containers unfold into plates? Does the word *bed* look like a *bed*?"

She squints. "Holy cow. Bed does look like a bed." She furrows her brow. "But when did takeout containers start unfolding?"

"Evidently, they always have. But they work better folded as far as I'm concerned."

"They work really well folded. So well that I don't know why anyone would unfold the container. But about your tent . . ."

I smirk because I can't resist the innuendo. My eyes stray to my crotch, and she blushes for a second.

"*Your tent.* The one you brought with you. You really have a tent in your pack?"

"Mia, I was a Boy Scout and then an Eagle Scout. You never know when you might need a tent, and I don't advise snoozing out in the open on public trails. Even if we're mostly alone." I gesture to the wildflower-filled meadow we've claimed as our own.

I reach into my pack, grab a pop-up beach tent, and unfold it, setting it up in less than three minutes. With avid interest, Mia watches the whole time, and even though I'm not doing something strapping like building a house or fixing a tire, I still like that she seems to dig that I'm handy. That I'm prepared. And that I have everything she's asked for. I tug on the end of the blanket, and she stands and hands it to me. I spread it on the floor of the tent.

"Ladies first." I gesture for her to go in.

"Such a gentleman."

As she lies down, all I can think is that she doesn't know the half of how gentlemanly I am being right now.

Because what I really want is to do ungentlemanly things to her as she curls up next to me in a tiny nap tent.

6

____

Conversations with the Cat
   Zeus

With a belly full of fish and a sun-warmed spot on the blanket, the cat was ready for yet another nap. He hadn't quite hit his full allotment of sleep for the day. He needed to catch up so he could be fully rested to sleep more tomorrow. The man was sound asleep, and the cat considered draping himself over his master's head. Surely, the man would sleep better with a cat wrapped around him. But then the woman flipped to her side, staring at him with big eyes. Was she going to stare him down? A cat?

Just try it.

But instead, she scratched between his ears.

Oh, baby. Do that again.

She obliged, stroking him more. He kicked up the noise box, purring at her.

"You're loud," she whispered under her breath.

Raising her hand, she scratched his chin. "You're mighty handsome."

Yep, keep it up.

"You're a perfect pair," she said, her eyes drifting from the feline to his master.

He rumbled louder, waiting for the woman to say more.

"A pair of lady-killers." She sighed as she stroked his back. "What's a woman to do?"

As she whispered, his feline thoughts drifted to a certain calico lady on the ninth story who might want to share a can of tuna with him at some point. He'd need to convince his master to take a trip on the elevator to her floor. He liked her whiskers. He liked her tail, too.

The woman's eyes drifted to the man, his chest rising and falling, the look on his face serene.

"If things were different . . ."

She sighed.

"Maybe then . . ."

She rubbed his furry belly.

"But I don't know how to make it all work."

So good. The rubbing was so good. He tuned out the woman's chatter, and eventually she stopped talking.

The man rustled, stretching his arms over his head, but still slept. The woman's eyes widened as the man's shirt rode up. Her breath seemed to catch as she stared at his stomach. Stared, and stared, and stared, as if it were a bird she wanted to devour.

Well, that made sense.

Birds were mighty tasty.

A few minutes later, the woman fell asleep, tangled up with the bird she wanted to eat.

7

———

Warm flesh presses to mine. Soft breath flutters in my ear. The body I most want to get my hands all over brushes against my side.

Torture. Exquisite torture.

My eyes snap open just like that—asleep to awake. Here I am, in the tent with Mia. One lovely, feminine leg is flung over mine, and a smooth, toned arm is draped over my stomach. Her eyelids flutter, and her lips twitch. She's on the edge of a dream, I suspect.

I don't move for several seconds. Instead, I let my imagination picture this moment unfolding again and again. Waking up next to Mia. Having permission to touch her. Being able to pull her close and take her in my arms.

Like she's done to me.

But that's something Dream Mia did. Not Awake Mia. No matter how enticing this scenario is, I force myself to focus on how it isn't reality.

The leg on mine? It means nothing.

The arm on me? It tells me zilch.

Turning my head, I scan for Zeus. He's staring at me, like he knows all my secrets.

Well, the dude does. Pets know everything. If cats and dogs could talk, man, the things they could spill.

I catch a flash of silver, and my eyes home in on the metallic glint. Oh hell. Mia's shirt is twisted, rising to her belly button, revealing a piercing—a simple silver barbell with a purple ball at the end. I'd like to say it's the sexiest thing on her body, but then I spot something hotter.

And cuter at the same damn time.

On her hip bone is a silhouette of a fox. The outline of the animal tattoo is unmistakable, from the pointy ears to the fluffy tail. It's about the size of a dime, one of the smallest pieces of ink I've ever seen.

This woman will be the death of all my restraint. I want to run my thumb over that tattoo so badly. To watch her body arch into that slight touch, and feel her tremble as I trace the lines of the tail.

I raise a hand, hovering it above her, tempted, so damn tempted.

Then she sighs, and a dart of *I don't want to get caught with my hand in the cookie jar* jolts me. I snatch my hand away, casually threading it through my hair and yawning.

"Just woke up," I say in my best groggy voice.

"Me, too." Her voice is gravelly, so sleepy-sexy.

Her eyes drift down, and she seems to realize she's tangled around me. "Oh, sorry."

"I didn't mind."

She slips her leg off me and then moves her arm. She stops at my stomach, patting it. "I like your snack baby."

I chuckle lightly.

"It's very . . . firm."

Jesus. That's not the only part of me that's firm. "Feel free to conduct a full test of firmness."

"As if your belly were a mattress?"

"Well, you do seem to be sleeping on me," I say, trailing off.

"Is it weird that I find you so comfortable?" she asks, her voice low and soft.

"I'm *normal* and *comfortable.* Would you also like to tell me I'm reliable?"

She twists her neck to look up at me, wiggling her eyebrows. "And punctual, too."

I roll my eyes. "Great. Just great."

Maybe it is great, though. Because her hand is still on my stomach. Her hand isn't moving. And I'm not moving, either. I lie perfectly still, watching her fingers splayed on my abs, picturing all the directions that hand could go. Up would be fine. No objections there. She should feel free to explore my pecs all she wants. But down? That'd be even better. I'd really like to see how her hand looks slipping under my shorts. Heading south. Wrapping around my—

Wait. That's not what I want.

Don't get me wrong—I do want to feel those soft hands all over my dick. But more than anything, I want to feel *her.* I want to touch that fox, then lick my way up her belly to her breasts, the hollow of her throat, her alluring neck. I want to roll over, slide on top of her, pin her wrists above her head, then tell her how badly I've wanted to have her beneath me since the night I met her at her brother's apartment.

And if she wants the same damn thing as I do, I know myself. I won't be satisfied with snacks of Mia. I'll need the full meal. Hell, I want the whole menu of Mia.

But the miles between us . . .

They loom so damn large. I've been around the block. I've dated. I've had serious girlfriends. And I've learned this—proximity matters. It's quite possibly the foundational element of a relationship. You need to be able to see each other. I don't want to rely on texts and phone calls. I want nights and mornings, and weekends, too. Maybe that makes me greedy, but I'm thirty-three, and I'm not interested in a fling anymore. I don't want a part-time woman. I'm ready to go all in.

How can we be all in with each other when we're on separate coasts? Sure, I spend time in California now and then for work, and a few months ago I was there even more. But I hired a West Coast tour manager, so I don't have too many reasons to jet out there every weekend.

Against all my desires, I sit up ramrod straight, and her hand slides off me. She brushes one against the other. I stare ahead at the opening of the pop-up tent. "We should go."

"Is it that late?"

I shake my head, checking out the sun patterns cast across the top of the tent. "I'm guessing it's a little after one. But we need to hike down, and you have your conference call."

She groans. "I should have canceled that call."

I laugh lightly, but I don't say *I told you so*. If she needs to do the call today, my job is to take her home. She straightens her shirt and gathers our supplies, minimal though they are.

We retrace our route, but this time we're faster, less chatty. We make no pit stops for hugs or deep conversations. We're all business, and I'm not sure if it's because I pushed her hand off me, or if we've simply talked ourselves out. Perhaps there's nothing left to say. Wouldn't that be great? Wouldn't it be absolutely wonderful to discover I have no more conversational bits and pieces to share with this woman? That's my new dream—that with this day I'll have exhausted my interest in her.

Then she won't have such a claim on my thoughts.

Inside the Jeep, Zeus curls up on the back seat and falls into slumber as I pull away from the trail, heading to the highway that'll take us back to the city.

"Patrick," she says after a few painfully silent miles.

I grip the wheel tighter. "Yeah?"

"Normal isn't a bad thing."

"That so?"

"Nor is comfortable."

"Really?"

"And reliable isn't, either."

"Yeah, I get that," I say with a heavy sigh. I still wish she'd chosen other adjectives.

She taps her bare fingernails against the dash. "I

dated this guy a year ago who always said he'd show up. But Zach was late. All the time. Sometimes when we'd made plans, he didn't show up at all."

I hate this Zach. "And?"

"I broke up with him."

"So you're looking for a punctual guy?" I ask, a flicker of hope inside me. I'm excellent at arriving on time.

She shakes her head. "That's not what I'm saying. And I'm not looking. I'm not out trolling for someone who'll show up at seven p.m. on the dot. I'm just saying . . ." She slows down, taking a beat, her voice the slightest bit wobbly. "I'm saying I like that you mean what you say. You do what you say. You show up."

"That seems a base level of acceptability, Mia," I say gently, but firmly, to get my point across. "Why should you, or my sister, or any woman, for that matter, feel like she should be happy if a guy merely keeps his word? Shouldn't we all do that?"

"Yes, of course," she says, her pitch rising. "But that's not what I'm trying to say."

"What are you trying to say?"

She blows out a long stream of air. "I'm saying normal is awesome. Normal is what we all want," she says, dragging her hand through her caramel-blond waves. "But it's hard to find. My God, you should see the guys out there."

For a flash, I picture her on a date with another guy, a nameless, faceless schmo, and my words come out harsher than I'd like. "Please, tell me more about the men you date."

She flinches, then snaps her gaze to me. "Wait. Are you jealous?"

Yes, I am. I'm jealous of Zach. I'm jealous of anyone who came before and anyone who'll come after Zach. I'm jealous of any guy who's taken her out for so much as a cup of motherfucking coffee.

After today—the things we shared, the jokes we told, the fears we laid bare—what is the point of keeping this treacherous ball of jealousy rolling around in my chest a secret? I should say yes. I should admit it.

I glance away from the road momentarily, meeting her gaze. And in her soft hazel eyes I see her kind spirit, her good heart, her wicked sense of humor. I relax my viselike grip on the wheel, the tension spilling out of me. I don't need to ruin our friendship with a misplaced admission.

"It's all good, Mia. Keep talking. About the normal thing," I say, keeping it calm, keeping it chill.

She clears her throat. "What I'm trying to say is I've met plenty of guys who are weird in all the wrong ways. Weird about commitment, weird about boundaries, weird about truth. I don't mean weird as in they have cute idiosyncrasies like constantly reciting the temperature inside a house."

I straighten my shoulders. "That's not weird. That's normal."

"It's something men do that I will never understand."

"I will never understand why women can't turn lights off when they go from room to room. You flick a switch," I say, miming turning off a light. "There.

Simple. And as for the temperature, we like to know precisely how hot or cold it is, so you'll have to try again on the 'not normal' thing."

She smirks. "You're missing the point. I'm trying to say that I like normal. A lot. The thing I want most is a normal guy."

I wait for her to continue. To reveal more. But she's quiet. She doesn't say she wants me—that I'm the normal guy she wants.

Maybe this is the moment of truth. This is what I need to get this dumb lust out of my system. In fact, today has been precisely what I needed. A cold dose of reality.

I flick on the right-turn signal, heading onto the bridge that'll take us back to Manhattan. I fiddle with the radio and tune in to a station that plays indie music. An upbeat song starts as the car rolls past the tolls and over the water.

For a flash, that primal fear of crashing into the sea lashes before my eyes, but the music shoves it out. I turn the dial a bit louder, and then Mia places her hand over mine.

I flinch briefly.

She turns my palm over and threads our fingers together.

My breath stops.

For several seconds, I don't even try to exhale. Nor do I tear my eyes from the road. Her fingers clasp mine, and finally, I relax into it.

There is no earthly reason why holding hands should feel this good.

But it does.

It feels better than good.

It's astonishing.

It stokes flames inside me, especially when she strokes my palm with her thumb. Every reason I recited in the tent—proximity, three thousand miles, different coasts—threatens to march back into my brain, but I tell them to scram. Right now, I want to feel her touching me.

I squeeze her hand as we cross the bridge. When we're on the other side, I steal a glance at her. She smiles at me, kind of sweet, kind of nervous, kind of like she likes this, too.

"Hey, Jackrabbit," I say.

She winks. "Hey, Kangaroo."

Right now, I'll take that nickname, thank you very much, even if it started from a douchey marsupial meme. I'll take it because she's holding my hand.

She doesn't let go. Not the rest of the way. Not till we reach the parking garage.

We separate, and I'm hit with how much I want to touch her again.

When we're inside the elevator, I press the button for the twentieth floor, then the twenty-fifth.

Once the doors close, she leans back against the opposite wall to me, her hands gripping the railing. "I liked holding your hand."

Zeus meows from his post on the floor, and I step closer to her. "It felt so *normal*," I say, using her favorite word.

Her eyes shine with desire. "It felt so good."

8

Like I said, proximity usually wins.

In this case, it's not only trumping the miles that often separate us, it's stomping all over any restraint I might once have had.

There are no miles now. This is a battle of inches. And I'm losing.

Gladly fucking losing, because my pulse races rocket-fast, and my skin is hot, just from being near her. "So, what do you think? You and me. Bad idea?"

She shakes her head. "Definitely not bad." She swallows. "Good idea?"

"Maybe the best idea?"

"Would it be?" she whispers.

"What do you think?"

She's breathing hard, and I love that. She licks her lips, her cheeks flushed. "Want to know what I think?"

"You know I do."

She lifts one hand and places it gently on my chest, pressing her fingers against my pecs. Even through my shirt, her touch triggers an instant response—a rush of desire to every molecule in my body.

"Sometimes I wish you still visited San Francisco," she says. "I liked it the few times I saw you out there."

We played pool one night when I flew into her hometown en route to a tour in Tahoe. Another time, I took her out to her favorite sandwich shop for a tomato and mozzarella panini for lunch, before I met the guy I've since hired as my West Coast manager. That's when I learned of her impressive appetite. Or, of how much bigger her eyes are than her stomach—that stomach I want to touch, and I have permission to at last. I run the tips of my fingers down the fabric covering her belly, and she gasps—a quiet but sensual little sound that leaves no room for argument. She's into this.

"I definitely wish you were in New York City more," I tell her, traveling to her arm, brushing my fingers down her bare skin. Goose bumps appear on her flesh, and she feels so good to touch. Her eyes flutter closed for a second, maybe more. When she opens them, those hazel irises are fiery with lust.

"I wish you weren't friends with my brother," she says, her tone unexpectedly dark. It gives me pause. I don't see why Max would be an issue. Not for us. Max isn't the type of guy to be a territorial asshat, and I'm not the type of guy he has to worry about with his sister.

"Why?" I raise an eyebrow in question.

Mia shakes her head. There's something she's not telling me. "It just makes it harder . . . and other reasons." She doesn't elaborate. I'm not sure I want her to right now. Not when we're both finally saying the things I've wanted to speak out loud and hear.

Besides, we know the score.

And yet, we're still here, barely any space between us, the elevator rising higher, dinging softly as it passes each floor.

"There are always reasons." I lift my hand to her hair, brushing it away from her face. She moves with me, her cheek following my palm, and the most desperate look crosses her eyes. Like she can't bear not to be touched right now. "But are those reasons more powerful than the fact that I'd really like to kiss you right now?"

My muscles relax, and heat shoots through me. It's a spectacular relief to give voice to how I feel, and a huge turn-on, too. Now she knows. We aren't playing poker anymore, holding our cards too close to the vest. I still don't know how much either one of us is willing to bet and willing to lose, but we're in the same card game.

She trembles, and her voice is feather soft and so inviting when she says, "Kiss me."

Hell to the yes.

I cup her cheek, rubbing my thumb across her skin, and it's as if she dissolves, as if she floats, and I can feel how incredibly mutual this attraction is.

However, she's also incredibly short.

I don't line up that easily with her. When I line my body to hers, my hard-on meets her navel. That's not the big issue—though it is *big*. The pressing issue is I'm more than a head taller. I dust a quick kiss to the top of her hair, laughing, to emphasize my point.

She laughs, too. "You're a foot taller."

"More than a foot." I lower my hands to her hips and lift her up, setting her ass on the bar in the elevator. She lets out a little squeal. Out of the corner of my eye, I see floor fifteen light up on the pad as we pass it.

This is going to be one fast kiss.

But I'll take it. I'm inches away from her soft, sensual lips. She parts them, and I close my eyes, dipping my mouth to hers, then the elevator slows.

On the seventeenth floor.

I groan and huff in frustration.

She winces, as if *not* kissing is as painful for her as it is for me.

The doors whisk open.

She slides off the bar, her feet hitting the floor as a fortyish-year-old woman strolls into the elevator, carrying several empty canvas grocery bags. She wears electric-blue glasses, and her black hair is twisted high in a bun. Earbuds blast some kind of loud music in her ears, and she clutches her phone, bopping along with it, and gives us a quick nod. When the doors close, she stabs the down button, then mutters under her breath, probably because she's realizing she entered an elevator going up.

I sigh heavily, because she's not even headed in the same direction as us. She doesn't even need this ride.

I look at Mia, right next to me. She brushes her hand over her hair, smoothing it out though I didn't get to mess it up like I wanted.

She shrugs and gives a *what can you do* smile as the elevator slows again, approaching my floor. Then she rises on tiptoe and dusts her lips along my jaw. Now it's my turn to shiver because . . . holy fuck. *Those lips.* I want to feel them all over me. I stare hard at her for the last two seconds of the ride, my eyes trying to say everything.

I want you so much.

The twentieth floor comes far too quickly, and I grab my backpack with my cat in it and give her a tip of the cap. "Time for your conference call, Jackrabbit. I don't want you to be late for it."

She smiles. "*Considerate.* You're considerate, too."

This time I take it as a compliment, because from Mia, I know it is.

9

———

I'd like to say that later we pick up where we left off, but that doesn't happen. Instead, I take off for a bike ride to burn all this excess energy, my version of taking a cold shower.

As I power along Hudson River Greenway on a titanium-grade custom bike that my buddy Carlos shipped to me, I weigh what to do next.

Well, the very next thing I'm required to do by the Competitive Guy Act is to pass the cyclist in front of me, which I accomplish with a quick burst of adrenaline, leaving the dude in the banana-yellow jersey ample opportunity to enjoy the view of my back tire.

With a clear path in front of me, I try to approach the Mia quandary like a trail I'm guiding some newbies along. Do I keep marching down this path? Or is it time to fork left and veer away from my preconceived notions of how a relationship should unfold?

The wild card, though, is her—her presence.

And that changes the game.

She's in town for the next eight days, and she's only five floors up from me. Theoretically, I could see her every day. We could start a crash course in whether we are a good idea or a bad idea. I could take her out every night, plan things I know she'd enjoy. Go all in for eight days. That has to be enough time for us to figure out what the hell to do with all this tension between us.

But as I shoot past another cyclist—I'll have to let Carlos know his custom ride, paired with some good old-fashioned energy, is a winning combo—I ask myself what actually changed this afternoon in the elevator.

Not that much, to be honest.

Logically, the only thing that has changed is information. I have evidence that she has the hots for me, too. Whoop-de-do. That doesn't fix the big hurdle between us—the motherfucking continent.

Or does it?

Do the miles truly matter?

I'd like to call my sister and ask her advice. Maybe find out if she's ever successfully set up a man and woman who live so far away from each other. Several weeks ago, Evie asked if there had ever been anything between Mia and me, saying she had seen the way I looked at her at the dinner party.

But my sister is away for the weekend with her new guy, and now that she's finally found a match of her own, I don't want to interrupt. I need to make this choice on my own. Is it worth pursuing something while Mia is here for the rest of the week?

As I burn off the rest of this lust, I feel I'm close to an answer.

But when I return home, the decision is snatched from me, courtesy of an SOS message from my East Coast manager.

Harvey has food poisoning! And the whitewater trip with Greenstone–Harrington Capital starts tomorrow afternoon.

My shoulders sag, and I drag a hand through my hair. Harvey is my most experienced guide. That means I just booked myself a trip out of town, and that also means there's no chance with Mia this week.

I write back to my manager and tell him I'll cover for Harvey. That's my job. I didn't start this company to sit at a desk and tell other people where to go, like an air-traffic controller. I started this company to be a pilot, flying the damn plane.

To be outside.

But ideally, not during the one damn week when the woman I want is in town. But so it goes.

I flop onto my couch with my pussycat in my lap and dial my buddy Carlos in California. "Your bike kicks ass," I tell him after he picks up. "I lapped twenty people, including Lance Armstrong look-alikes."

He chuckles. "Only the finest for you. And how are the other models working out for your business?" he asks, since I've stocked his more economically priced models for the bike tours we recently launched.

"The customers love them. A few have even said they want to buy one, so maybe you'll let me use that cabin of yours in Blue Canyon next time I'm in California. It can be my commission."

"Ha. I loan it to no one. That's my baby."

I snap my fingers. "Shucks. I wish there were something I could do to convince you. Like, say, buying another dozen of your bikes for the East Coast, too."

He's silent for a few seconds. Then he clears his throat. "What did I say? I believe I said you can use it on your next Tahoe trip."

I grin, and stretch my arms across the back of the couch. "Excellent."

When I end the call, I spot a text from Mia, and my heart bounces around in my chest like a tennis ball. I have it bad.

Mia: At dinner. Still thinking about good ideas and bad ideas. How about you?

Patrick: Ideas are all I can think about. Have you landed one way or the other?

Mia: I've landed on, I hope that woman's groceries were absolutely delicious for making us miss a chance in the elevator.

Patrick: Yeah, me, too. Feel free to stop by later.

My finger hovers above the last message for a few more seconds. Finally, I hit send, even if it might be a little too pushy, a little too suggestive.

Maybe it is, since her reply is straight down the middle of the *I can't read it* road.

Mia: I wish I could. The dinner is running late. But we're having fun!

I rub my hand over the back of my neck and heave a sigh. I want to tell her I'll wait up. But that sounds really fucking lame. And that's not where we are— we're not hovering in *I'll wait up for you* territory.

In fact, we're not anywhere at all on the relationship road map.

We're back to where we were yesterday. Friends who've never kissed.

10

—————

Zeus meows his displeasure as I head for the door.

His green eyes narrow as he unleashes a needy, distrustful meow that loosely translates into *what on earth could possibly be more enticing out there than spending time with me in here?*

I kneel and scratch his chin. "Dude, I'm sorry. I have to go."

Another wounded mewl makes it clear how abhorrent he finds the idea of my departure.

But that chin rub is so good he emits a little rumble, even though it's clearly against his will.

"You'll be fine. Daisy will visit you twice a day to give you food," I say, reminding him that his favorite cat-sitter will pop by for regular visits. "You love her."

His tail twitches like it does when he's annoyed I haven't fed him yet, when a bird is on the other side of the glass, and when I leave for a trip.

"I'll be back in a few days." I scratch between his

ears. He arches his back and cranks up the volume. I'm forgiven. For a second.

In the elevator, I check my phone and find a missed message from last night.

From Mia.

It's a picture of the douchey kangaroo she mentioned, only she's edited the meme. The kangaroo has boobs now and is wearing a white bikini and red lipstick. The caption reads in blocky white letters: "Hey, guy, wanna see my pouch?"

I laugh hard, right from the gut.

Jesus.

It's raunchy and goofy at the same damn time.

I peer closer at the time. She sent it after midnight. And I have half a mind to analyze what that means.

But I don't.

Sometimes a meme is just a meme.

And sometimes a kiss never happens, and not even a kangaroo in drag can change the score.

Besides, she's busy. Hell, I'm busy, too. It's all for the best that the grocery lady came between us. Now, Mia and I can remain as we've always been. *Friends.* And we'll always stay friends. This most excellent photo of a drag queen kangaroo is proof that we're better off as buddies.

There are other fish in the sea. Hell, my own sister is a matchmaker. She might very well know someone. But when I reach the lobby and stride to the glass doors that open to the sidewalk, *the* woman I want to be with is running toward me.

She wears neon-green running shorts and a form-fitting white tank top. That is all.

Well, running shoes, of course. But I'm not lingering too long on the shoes. I'm looking at her trim body, those toned arms, her shapely legs, and then, my favorite part—her face. Her gorgeous, beautiful face, all rosy-cheeked from a morning run.

She beams when she sees me and practically rips her earbuds from her ears.

"Good morning," she says with a cheery, infectious smile.

The corners of my lips curve up. "It is a good morning, indeed. What are you listening to?"

"A podcast." She flashes the screen at me, and it's a business-centric show.

I nod. "Ah, back in all-business mode?"

She narrows her eyes and wags her finger at me. "Yes, but it's good because . . ." She lifts her arms and chants "ahhh," as if she's an angel sent from on high to issue a heavenly pronouncement. "I had an epiphany."

"Oh yeah?"

She drops her arms and pokes my chest. "You were right. Stepping away from work cleared my head. All these ideas for where to go next with Pure Beauty came rushing in." She adds a *whoosh* sound effect like a stream.

I raise an eyebrow, intrigued. "Really?"

"Yes, really! I swear, Patrick. Everything came together for me yesterday in a mad rush. Then it crystallized last night."

"Like new product lines and stuff?"

"Maybe," she says, a little coyness to her tone.

"Ah, I know. It's beauty products for cats, right?"

"Absolutely," she says, in mock seriousness. She strokes her cheek. "It'll make their fur even softer." She notices the gear in my hand and on my back and stops to stare at my bags, then at me. "Do you have a tour?"

I nod. "That I do."

Her smile disappears. Her lips turn into a sad line. "For how long?"

"Most of the week."

"You're not around the next few days?"

I shake my head. "I'll be back in time for the wedding."

"Wow," she says under her breath, as if she's been thrown for a loop. Her reaction intrigues me, makes me wonder if she wanted me around. But before I can noodle on that, she seems to find her bearings. "What about Zeus? Do you need me to feed him?"

I smile. "He has a regular cat-sitter." I cross my index and middle fingers. "He and Daisy are like that."

Her mouth drops into a full-on frown. An absolutely magnificent pout. "*Please.* I want to spend time with him. He's so cute. Let me do it. I'll be here all week." She makes the sign of the cross on her chest. "And I swear I won't look through your medicine cabinet."

I laugh. "You are more than welcome to check out my toothpaste and deodorant. It's Crest and the Trader Joe's brand."

"You spoiled the surprise," she says, stomping her foot. She screws up one corner of her lips as if she's plotting something nefarious. "Well, there's always your fridge."

"Condiments, Jackrabbit. Condiments as far as the eye can see. All the mustard varieties in the world are at your disposal. But feel free to paw around in my boxer briefs drawer."

She wiggles her eyebrows. "Is your high school yearbook there?"

I sigh. "Mia, I didn't keep a copy of it, and you just made sure that Daisy will remain my sitter."

She parks her hands on her hips. "I promise I'll be good. I really want to help you, since you helped me immensely yesterday. And I like the . . . *pussycat*," she says, tiptoeing and leaning close to my ear. Just like that, with her body near me, her dirty words on my neck, I give in.

"Fine. You can feed him. I'll text Daisy and let her know I have it covered, and I'll get you a key."

She claps her hands. "Excellent." Then her smile burns off. "About last night . . ."

I wave a hand dismissively. I need to get in the zone before this rafting trip. No need to bring any baggage over what didn't happen. "Don't worry about it."

"The picture?"

"No," I say slowly, pointing behind me to the building. "The elevator, right?"

"Sure. The elevator."

"It's fine. No big deal," I say, keeping it light and easy. Casual even. "We're friends, right? It's all good."

She blinks as if she's startled. "Right. Friends." Each word comes out at the speed of molasses. She sounds sad about that prospect, but isn't that what we are? We almost kissed, and then she didn't come over later. No big deal. It happens. The elevator was a blip, a moment in time. Now, we need to be friends again. Friends who've never kissed.

"You're taking care of my cat. We're clearly friends."

She smiles, but it's a kind I've never seen on her before. A smile I can't read. "We're totally buds." She smacks my shoulder like a dude would do.

I head back inside, grab my spare key from the concierge desk, and hand it to her, along with instructions on feeding the cat. Then, I remember one last detail.

"My suit is coming back from the cleaners on Wednesday. They'll deliver it, but any chance you can grab it from the concierge? I don't like to leave things there too long. Those guys are pretty busy and deliveries pile up."

"I'll grab it, no problem. You spent your day off with me yesterday. The least I can do is get your suit and feed your cat." She smiles again, that same unrecognizable variety, before she adds, "It's what a friend would do."

Ah, got it. It's the *friend* smile. It's clear that's what we're going to be. That must be what she's preferred all along.

Good thing I have the next four days on the raging waters to reset our relationship to the friend zone.

11

———

Conversations with the Cat
  Zeus

It was days later.

Or, really, it might have been hours. His belly was convinced it was longer. He'd tried in vain to find a mouse, even a mole. He honestly wouldn't mind a moth for a small snack, either. But the place he lived remained as fastidious and mouse-free as it had ever been.

Fortunately, as the sun dipped in the sky, the door creaked open.

At last.

Someone had remembered the cat existed. Surely, it would be the red-haired woman with the jingly bracelets on her arms. That woman was a favorite person of his. She seemed to have one purpose in the world.

Serve him.

He liked it when humans had that purpose.

But that woman didn't wander in. It was the bird woman. The woman who wanted to nibble on the man he lived with.

Well, hello, lady.

The cat rubbed against her leg both in greeting and a clear command—*FEED ME NOW.*

"So good to see you, too." She bent down to stroke his head. "I've missed you so much. I'll be taking care of you for the next few days. But I promised Patrick I would be a very good girl. So if you see me rifling through his things, you have permission to scratch and claw me."

She was taking too long. He needed food, and he needed it stat. He'd have to try her other leg. Perhaps rubbing that one would activate the can opener.

"Oh, you're too sweet. Do you want me to pick you up?"

The woman scooped him in her arms, and he pushed his head against the bare skin of her chest. Ah, that was nice. No wonder his master seemed fascinated with that area of the woman.

"I'll give you your tuna, and I'll tell you all about the exciting things I'm working on."

She set him down, and he paced across the tile, waiting, waiting, waiting, as she entered the feeding zone. The sound of metal opening metal rang out like a joyous song. Food was coming at last.

He turned in ceremonious circles, round and round, unable to contain his sheer excitement.

She set the dish on the floor, and he nearly wept with feline ecstasy—tuna and kibble. He purred as he ate. Meanwhile, the woman perched on the counter, kicking her feet, chattering on and on, perhaps to him.

"So that's what I want to do with Pure Beauty. Because beauty products for cats is such a brilliant idea, right, Zeus? We can call it Purr Beauty then." She stopped and winked at him, then hummed. "But then, there's the other issue. What about Eric?" she asked, and her tone shifted. It was the sound of frustration, like how he felt when there was no longer a warm body on the bed in the morning. "I have to tell him about what happened with Eric. But I don't want to go there, because this doesn't seem remotely the same. The way I feel for Patrick is completely different. It's like night and day." She sighed and went quiet for a spell. "But I know it'll have to come up. I need to be upfront about what's held me back. Don't you think?"

After he finished his feast, the woman stayed with him a little longer. He rewarded her excellent can-opening skills by deigning to sit in her lap as she tapped away on her little silver machine, chatting on the phone with someone she called Felicia and someone else she referred to as Lisa.

When she arrived another time, she carried a bag with her. "Look, Zeus. It's a suit. Isn't it to die for?" The woman ran a hand down the covering, almost as if she were worshipping the item. He rubbed against the bag, too. He was unable to resist clothing in bags. Or bags in general for that matter. "Seeing Patrick in this suit might possibly make me ovulate. I swear, I can't be held responsible for my actions. Wait. Wait. Of course I'm responsible. I have to be good. Must be good. Even though that body in that suit might very well be the ever-loving death of my restraint."

She walked into the other room, and he trotted after her instantly, since she seemed to have forgotten his needs.

A meow here and there and he'd successfully lured her back to the kitchen where she opened a can and fed him, then rattled on and on.

"I wonder what tie he'll wear. If he'll need help straightening it. If he'll need help taking it off."

He had his own issues to noodle on as he devoured the feast—was trout tastier than salmon? Was mackerel better than yellowtail? Those were interesting questions he contemplated as he dined.

She hopped off the counter, stared at the shiny fridge, and shook a finger at herself. "Stop it. Just stop it. You know the risks. Too high. Besides, he just wants to be friends. It doesn't matter if you want to straighten his tie or undo it."

Her stomach rumbled, and the cat really thought she ought to spend more time focusing on hunting her prey. The woman opened the box that held human food, grabbed a small bottle, and kissed his furry head before she left.

Sometime after, the man returned, and the cat circled his ankles in excitement.

"Hey, buddy, did Mia take good care of you? Did she treat you well? Did she tell you all her secrets?"

His answer was a deep and satisfied purr.

He was the cat. That meant he knew all their secrets, but he would never tell.

12

─────────

After a hot shower to wash off the day, I run a towel over my hair, dry off, and pull on a pair of black boxer briefs. I stroll into the kitchen and yank open the fridge, just in case something miraculously appeared inside it while I was gone.

Nope.

Still full of condiments and beer. Though they are the two basic food groups, some protein would be nice. I pick up my phone to place an order for a burger, and a message from Mia lands on my screen.

Four days in the woods, four days away from the woman I want. That was absolutely enough time to recalibrate my feelings back to *just friends*.

I exhale deeply before I open her text. Remind myself of who she has to be to me.

Mia, my friend. Mia, who I put in the friend zone. Mia, who I've never kissed, and never will kiss.

I read her text. It's a reply to my earlier text message

letting her know I'd returned and she was relieved of cat detail.

Mia: Welcome back! I loved every second of cat detail. Also, if you're wondering where the sriracha is, I might have borrowed it. But I'm on my way to return it right now.

Patrick: Good. I was hungry. Now I'll be satisfied with some sriracha.

Mia: It is quite filling.

I set the phone down, pleased that we both executed that *just friends* exchange so easily. It's going to be seamless slipping back into friendship with her.

Two minutes later, she raps on my door. "Damn, you're fast," I say as I unlock and open it.

And it's safe to say her jaw drops.

Her eyes approximate the size of pizza pies as she swallows hard, as if there's something stuck in her throat.

"I think you forgot to put on clothes . . ." She points at me with the sriracha in her hand.

Oh, yeah. I'm wearing only my boxer briefs. I wiggle my eyebrows. "Good thing I didn't slip into a yellow thong tonight."

She furrows her brow. "Please tell me you don't own a thong."

"You tell me. Zeus said you went through my drawers."

"Oh my God. I did not. I swear."

I hold up my hands in surrender. "Just teasing." I open the door all the way. "Come in. I was about to order a burger. Are you hungry?"

I pat myself—*virtually*—on the back for staying in the zone.

"Is that a rhetorical question?"

"Does that mean you want one?"

She flubs her lips. "Do high heels hurt? Are meetings the bane of my existence? Does cereal taste better with milk?"

I laugh. "Gee. I don't really know if high heels hurt."

"They do. They're the devil, and yes, I want a burger. Veggie, please, with cheddar."

"Coming your way."

I open my Seamless app, place the order from my favorite diner, drop my phone on the coffee table, and then offer her a beer. She takes it and tips the neck to mine in a toast. "To your return." Then her eyes wander, traveling over my frame as I lean against the kitchen counter. "Are you going to put on any clothes?"

I decide to have fun with her. That's what friends do. Plus, I'm not lacking in the confidence department. I wasn't always in great shape. Fitness is an effort, so I'm not going to pretend I don't like looking this way. "Do you want me to get dressed, Mia? Does it make you uncomfortable to see all this masculinity on display?"

She closes her eyes for a second. "It's fine. You can wear those things."

"Things?"

"Those form-fitting boxers that show off your fantastic ass," she blurts out. "There. Are you happy I said it?"

I peer behind me as if checking out my own butt. "Damn, that is one fine ass. Did you want to conduct any firmness tests on it?"

She drops her face into her hands, laughing. When she looks up, she slides the sriracha to me along the counter. "Here you go." Next comes the key. "And I picked up your suit."

Good. Come sit on my face now.

Shit. Where did that come from? I shake away the filthy thought that flashed before my eyes. "You're pretty much a perfect cat-sitter."

She smiles. "So how was the trip?"

I tell her about the group from the financial firm, and how they were an interesting mix of daring and cautious, but that kind of reflected the point of the trip. "These two firms just merged, and the company wanted to bring the new team members together. Have them work in tandem on the rapids."

She arches a brow. "That's kind of cool. Did it help them bond, or what have you?"

I nod. "I think so. At the beginning, you could sense some tentativeness. Maybe even wariness. But after the first day on the water, they were getting along better. By the time we navigated the toughest sections, it was as if they'd been working together for years."

"That's amazing. You're like glue."

"I'm very sticky, Mia," I say straight-faced.

She laughs. "That's kind of gross and sexy at the same time."

"That's generally what I aim for." We make our way to my couch where we sink onto the soft maroon cushions.

She takes a sip of beer and sets her bottle on the coffee table. "So I guess this is how it goes. You're comfortable enough around me to drink beer in your underwear."

I laugh, leaning back into the couch and stretching an arm over the top of it. My reboot completely worked. Even she can tell we're awesome at being buddies. "I guess I am."

As I take a drink, she looks at me. Studies me. Stares.

"What is it?"

She licks her lips. "I'm sorry, but you have a perfect body."

It's like an injection of pride right in my chest. "You really don't have to apologize for saying that. Also, so do you."

Crap. I didn't mean that in a friendly way at all.

A reddish tint spreads in her cheeks. "You really do." She flaps her hands around at me, gesturing. "Your abs. Your arms. Your biceps. I think your biceps are bigger than my thighs."

"Possibly." Setting down my beer, I take her hands, and bring them both around my left bicep. She can't touch her fingertips, and naturally, this pleases me to an incomprehensible degree.

"Holy guns," she says, kind of breathless.

Then I move her hands and circle them around her thigh. She's wearing jeans. I keep my hands on hers as her fingertips touch.

"Do I get to touch your thighs now and compare them to my tiny arm?" she asks, a hint of mischief in her hazel eyes.

In an instant, my bearings are gone. I don't know where we are anymore. I don't know how we slipped so quickly into this touchy, flirty game, but I know I like it. I know I want it.

"Go for it," I tell her.

She wraps her right hand around her opposite arm, coming a few inches shy of her fingers touching her thumb. Then, she places that same hand on my thigh, barely covering the top of it.

I laugh at how small her hand is on my body. Then I stop laughing because it's *her* hand on my thigh, and now I know exactly where we are. We're no longer in the friend zone. Friends don't touch each other's thighs like this. This is elevator land.

While I was in the woods, I tried to put her in the friend zone. I tried hard, and I thought I'd succeeded. Maybe I was just fooling myself.

But there's no fooling myself now.

Sometimes you don't know where a trail goes, but you turn onto it anyway. Like she did to me in the car, I set my hand on top of hers. I'm not lying when I say it's an instant turn-on. This woman—she has my number.

She has to know it, too, as I curl my fingers through hers.

The barest hitch in her breath tells me she's turned on, too. Neither one of us is wandering in the friend zone right now.

Thank God.

When I raise my face and meet her eyes, she asks, "Were you always in such perfect shape?"

I laugh. "I was born with muscles. I sprang out of the womb lifting weights."

"Seriously. Have you always been so . . . fit?"

My smile fades away. "No."

"Why do you say it like it's sad?"

"It's not sad. It's just true. In my freshman year of high school I was—"

"Chubby?" she supplies with a lift of her eyebrow, like she can't quite believe that.

I shake my head.

"Skinny?"

I make a rolling gesture. "And?"

Her eyes bug out. "And awkward?"

I flash a huge grin at her, baring my teeth.

"With braces?"

"Forever," I say. "That was the kind I had. The forever kind of braces. I swear they were on for my entire high school years and only came off a month before graduation."

She stares at me in disbelief. "I can't picture you skinny and awkward."

I hold up a finger to correct her. "Tall, skinny, and awkward."

She pats my shoulder with her free hand. "I'm going to need to see the photos."

"Why?"

"I can't see you as anything but what you are now."

"So, what's wrong with that? Why do you want to?"

She tucks a strand of hair behind her ear. "I don't know. Maybe there's a part of me that likes knowing you weren't always this . . ."

"Handsome? Strapping? Studly?" I ask, puffing out my chest as I exaggerate preening for her.

"Yes," she says, squeezing my fingers more tightly, sending heat all over my skin. "Can I see?"

"I don't have my yearbook," I remind her. "But I have a picture that Evie sent me recently." Without letting go of her hand, I reach for my phone then open the text thread from my sister, searching for a digital shot she snapped of a framed photo of us she came across at our parents' house.

She titled it *Before We Were Cool* and sent another text that read, "Just kidding. We were never cool."

"There am I, in all my TSA glory. That's tall, skinny, awkward to you, Jackrabbit," I say as I show her the pic. My sister wears big round glasses and is sticking her tongue out, and I tower above her, a muscle-free metal-mouth.

Mia doesn't laugh. She smiles, then sighs, then nibbles on the corner of her lips. "I love it," she whispers.

And I crack up. "You're such a goofball. Why on earth would you like this?" I toss the phone to the table.

"Because it means you're—"

I hold up my hand. "Don't say normal again."

"Tell me what changed, why you're no longer TSA."

"My parents sent me to summer camp my freshman year. I'd already been a Boy Scout and an Eagle Scout, but this was every day. Outdoors. I fell in love with the swimming, the hiking, the canoeing, the rafting, and the obstacle courses. I couldn't get enough of it. I came home fifteen pounds heavier."

She runs her other hand down my bicep. "This kind of heavy?"

"Yeah," I say, and the word comes out dry, husky.

She's turned the temperature in me to red-hot. She draws her hand down my pecs, to my abs. "You're so . . ."

"So what?"

"Every part of you is hard."

I laugh, and my eyes drift to my crotch. "Yes."

She takes notice of the tent in my briefs and licks her lips.

"And that's because of you," I say, my voice lower but my words clear. She's been complimenting me, but I need her to know how I feel. Turns out four days away from her didn't reset anything at all. I don't know where we're headed tonight. I don't know where we're going. All I know is I can't turn back. "Because of what you do to me. Because of your body, your face . . . *you*."

She takes a breath, her lips parting. "This is so..." she whispers.

"It's not."

My gaze strays to her wandering fingers, traveling down my arm, over my elbow to my wrist. My little Mia is such the explorer, and it's me she wants to discover. She looks at me like she wants to touch me everywhere. Lick my skin. Run her fingers all over me.

She looks at me the way I look at her.

Screw friends.

Screw distance.

Screw the hurdles.

I'm going all in.

13

I let go of her hand and thread my fingers through her hair. "Get on me."

Then I grab her hips and move her so she's straddling my lap. She gasps, a sexy noise that turns into a moan as she sinks down on my hard-on.

I hiss because it feels so fucking good.

"I wanted to come over the other night. After dinner. After the elevator," she blurts out.

"Yeah?"

She nods. "Dinner ran late, but I couldn't stop thinking about you."

"What were you thinking?"

"That we didn't get to kiss, and I wanted to so badly."

"I can fix that problem right now."

I take her face in my hands and bring her to me. Then the world spirals away as I kiss Mia Summers for the very first time.

It's extraordinary. Her lips brush against mine, and

she wastes no time. She slides closer, rubbing on my dick as she presses her chest to me. It's as if she's climbing me, and God, how I want this. How I want her like this.

I thread my fingers through her hair, pulling her closer, kissing her deeper. Tasting her. Her mouth is soft and sweet, and she makes these little sounds—whimpers, sighs, gasps—that make me nearly lose my mind.

I'm kissing Mia. She's on my lap, rubbing against my erection, kissing me as if her every last breath depends on it. Her tongue tangles with mine, and in a hot second, the kiss become furious. Greedy. Like two people who are mad about each other. I curl my hands around her head, wanting to get as close as I can, but she bats them away.

I break contact for a moment and raise a questioning eyebrow.

"My turn." She lifts her hands, cups my cheeks, and then she strokes my jaw. Reverently. Hungrily. And I know what she's doing. She's feeling my beard. She's touching my stubbled jaw with eager fingers, as if she's wanted to get her hands on me for as long as I've wanted to touch her.

I don't stop her. I drop my hands to her hips, and I guide her along, moving her so she grinds against my cock, and she's gasping and murmuring as she kisses me.

We consume each other. We are ravenous. My brain turns to static, firing pleasure signal after pleasure signal to every nerve in my body. I want to live in this moment for the rest of the night. I don't ever want to forget how good it feels not only to kiss her, but to be kissed by her.

She rocks harder, goes faster, murmurs louder, then she separates and looks at me with desperate eyes. "You have no idea."

I shake my head. "I do. I have every idea."

And when I pull her back to me, ready to kiss the breath out of her once more, my phone rings.

I groan.

"Ignore it," she whispers.

"It's the diner, probably. Burgers."

She wiggles her eyebrows. "Well, in that case . . ."

She rolls off me as I answer the phone.

"Good evening, Mr. Milligan. We have a delivery from Wendy's Diner."

"Send him up, please, Trevor."

"No problem. Also, sir, you have a few packages that arrived this week. Do you want me to bring them up, too?"

That must be some new gear I ordered—goodies I wanted to test before we add them to the lineup. "Sure. The more the merrier."

"And finally," he says. "I have a plant delivery for a Mister Zeus."

I furrow my brow. "Plant delivery?" Then I shrug. "Bring it all up. We'll make it a party."

When I end the call, I notice my erection has had the courtesy to subside. Shame, since it was a particularly good one.

I stand. "I should get dressed."

"Undressed worked for me," Mia says with a little twitch in her lips, but she's not looking at me. She's tapping away on her phone. "Hold on. I need to deal with something from Lisa."

"Who's Lisa?" I ask as I head to my bedroom, since I don't want to be the douche who answers the door nearly free-range for anyone but Mia.

"My VP of products."

When I return a minute later, dressed in jeans and a T-shirt, her head is crooked to the side, and she's talking on the phone.

"Right. But what if we move up that date, too?" she asks then holds up her finger to let me know she'll be done soon.

I nod, scoop up the two empty beer bottles, and put them in the recycling bin in my kitchen.

"So it looks like that would work then? Can Felicia do it, too?" Mia asks, as someone knocks on the door.

I open it and take the food from the diner delivery guy, thanking him and giving him a tip from the app. After I put the food on the counter, Trevor's at the door, laden with boxes from REI and a small potted plant with a silvery bow around the terra-cotta.

I give it the side-eye, but there's a card on it.

"Here you go," Trevor says, and I tip him, place the boxes on the floor, and hold up the plant quizzically.

When Mia sees it, her eyes widen, and she mouths *that's from me.*

Then into the phone, she says, "Hey, can I call you back in two minutes?"

And that tells me all I need to know. The evening activity is over.

She hangs up and gestures to the plant. "I ordered a little gift for Zeus. To thank him for being such a good companion. Want to let him sniff it?"

And I can't be annoyed. "You got him catnip?"

She crinkles her nose, her dimples in full force. "I did. Is that okay? He's not allergic to catnip, is he?"

I laugh. "He's not allergic to anything," I say, glancing to the sleeping king, who's chosen the TV stand as his evening nap spot.

She presses her hands together. "I feel terrible, but I really have to deal with this call. It's only five on the West Coast."

"Go," I say with a smile, picking up the box with her veggie burger and handing it to her. "Cat beauty calls."

She smiles. "It does." She takes a deep breath. "I'll see . . ."

"I'll see you at the wedding," I say, finishing for her. I've just spent the last four days putting Mia back in the friend zone, and now I've gladly jumped back to elevator land with her in mere minutes.

But I need to figure out what the hell to do with the big problem. The problem I can't fix. The miles. I need the time to process what the hell all this means.

Other than the obvious.

She's trying to get my cat high.

14

———

The Rolling Stones' "Beast of Burden" bounces from the old sound system at Joe's Sticks as the groom misses an easy shot.

"Damn," Chase says, shaking his head as he regards the pool table disdainfully, then his hands. "Where did my hand-eye coordination go? I can't believe anyone lets me operate on them with these hands."

"Time to turn your license in," his best bud, Wyatt, says from across the green felt.

"Or maybe"—I lean against my pool cue—"Chase could be throwing the game on purpose."

Chase laughs, dragging a hand through his light brown hair. "Yeah, you guys are cramping my style by bringing me here."

"Tell the truth, Dr. Summers," Wyatt says, his blue eyes narrowing, his tone toughening as if he's trying to shake him down.

Max makes his way around the table, lining up a shot.

Joe's is our regular haunt. Good friends, good beer, and a few competitive rounds of pool are an ideal trio before we send Chase down the aisle tomorrow. I came here directly from work, and it has been a day, cramming in not only my segment on first aid in the woods for WRBC Channel 10, but also a meeting with Dana, our reservations manager, to review some upcoming trips, including some potential ongoing clients. Those are some of my favorite kinds, and as we assigned leaders for the tours, I told her which ones I wanted to handle myself. I signed off on the employee handbook, too, and boy, am I glad that our rules have tightened now. That's a huge weight off my shoulders.

Oh, but that's not all. Mia and I texted on and off throughout the day. She told me the bridesmaids are taking Josie to see *Hamilton* tonight as a surprise, since Josie's been dying to see it, and Mia planned to throw her bra at the stage during the curtain call, since it was a bachelorette party, after all.

I've no doubt that's precisely what the theater likes its patrons to do, I'd replied.

Good thing it's showtime at the musical, otherwise I'd be tempted to check for a message from her. Doing that with Max nearby feels all kinds of wrong. Though, truth be told, feeling the way I do and *not* telling him feels all kinds of wrong, too.

Spencer takes a swallow from his beer then sets the bottle down. "What could be better than the six of us? Half of us are married, with one more to go tomorrow, and Max on deck in another few months, while Wyatt already has a kid at home."

At the end of the table, Nick pushes his glasses up the bridge of his nose. "Not to mention, one third of us have pregnant wives."

"Hear, hear. To my soon-to-be-born son," Spencer says, raising his beer, then tipping it in Nick's direction. "And my soon-to-be-born nephew, even though it's still a weird concept that *you're* going to be related to *my* nephew."

"Yeah, I'll just be, ya know, his father," Nick deadpans. Spencer's wife, Charlotte, is due in a month, and Harper, Nick's wife and Spencer's little sister, isn't far behind.

Spencer shakes his head, as if this is all too much to digest. "Still strange that you're married to my sister."

"Speaking of sisters, how's Mia doing?" Wyatt asks, directing his question at Chase and Max. "Natalie and I didn't see her much this week."

"She's been running around for work," Chase answers.

"Building her business has been pretty all-consuming," Max adds, looking at Chase.

Something seems to pass between them. Absently, I scratch my jaw, wondering what it is.

Then, my conscience nags at me. I need to let Max know what's going on, and I'm not talking about that hot-as-sin kiss on the couch last night. I've been doing a lot of thinking lately, and I've come to a decision. I need to tell him what's in my heart for her, and that needs to happen ASAP. Maybe even tonight. I'll have to search for the right moment.

A little later, Max clears his throat and raises his

beer bottle in a toast. "To my brother, Chase. The happiest guy around. Josie is perfect for you, and we've always known it. I'm thrilled that you're marrying her, and may you always be not just the happiest guy around—but even happier."

Chase looks almost embarrassed, but also ridiculously delighted. The dude is, quite simply, madly in love with his bride.

Wyatt claps slowly. "To the golden boy. May your life with my sister always be golden."

Nick lifts his beer. "I'll second that, since Josie's my sister, too."

Spencer nods from Chase to Nick. "You two should form a club. The Society for Dudes Who Fell for Their Friend's Sisters."

Max laughs. "Don't even think of looking at me. Henley is related to none of you fuckers."

"Nor is Charlotte." Spencer's eyes land on me. "And what about you, Captain Outdoors? Are you the next one?"

I force out a laugh then take a hearty gulp of my beer to hide the fact that he's nailed it, whether he knows it or not.

Max shakes his head, chuckling. "Guys. It's Chase's night. Let's keep it that way."

And that ends my search for an opening. Tonight is not the time to tell Max that I absolutely want to be the next one in the club.

15

———

I stroll across one of the bridges in Central Park, on my way to the wedding at the boathouse. When I reach the steps heading to the ceremony, I spot a familiar silhouette in the crowd of guests milling about in front of the doors. A blond woman, wearing a sky-blue dress, is chatting with a couple. When she finishes her conversation, I call Evie's name.

She whirls around and waves when she sees me.

"Fancy meeting you here," I say as I reach her. Her date and some of our mutual friends are chatting a few feet away.

"And you. What a surprise," she teases as she throws her arms around me. I bend lower and give her a bear hug.

"How many weddings a year is it for you now?"

"This would be my tenth in the last twelve months," she says with a note of pride.

"And of those, how many are because of you?"

"Five," she says, beaming.

We high-five each other. "You are the Queen of Love. And when will yours be?" I ask, my gaze drifting pointedly to her date, a brainiac Internet genius who makes her so damn happy. Dylan's talking with his sister.

Evie blushes and lowers her voice cautiously. "I'm not sure, but I have a feeling he's been ring shopping."

"He knows a damn good thing when he sees it."

Evie steps closer and adjusts my purple tie, knotting it tighter. "I swear, it's like men never know how to tie these. You spend so much time in shorts. And what about you?"

"What about me? Do I know how to tie a tie? I believe I do," I say with a smirk.

She gently swats me. "I mean, what about you and Mia?"

I let a smile cross my lips. Evie's bright blue eyes—the same shade as mine—twinkle with excitement. The last time she asked me about Mia, nothing had happened between us. And while I'm not one to kiss and tell, I do want my sister's advice.

I cup her elbow and gently guide her away from the other guests. "Listen, I need to ask something, Ev. Have you ever known a couple in a long-distance relation-ship where it worked?"

She beams. "Yes. Silly. Is that why you've held back with Mia?"

I shrug. "Kind of."

"And now?" Her voice is laced with excitement.

"Well, I know she's into me. I'm not sure if it's to the

same degree, but I guess I'm tired of pretending I'm not completely—"

"Besotted with her?"

I point a finger at her in acknowledgement. "Guilty as charged."

She claps her hands and bounces on her toes. "I knew it. I knew it all along. And no, I don't think it's ridiculous to pursue something with someone who lives far away. Yes, I think it's absolutely harder. I won't kid you about that. But it happens. It's real. Sometimes you fall in love with someone who lives halfway around the world." My sister's eyes turn dreamy.

"Mia isn't halfway around the globe," I point out.

Evie arches an eyebrow. "But the other part?"

"What part? The falling part?"

"Falling in—" She stops, her voice going softer. "The most important question is this—how would you feel if you never took the chance to let her know you wanted a relationship, damn the miles between you?"

"How would I feel . . ." I repeat, musing on the words.

An usher dings a bell, and that ends the conversation. It's time to head inside the boathouse and take our seats. A sign reads, "This is an unplugged ceremony. Please turn off your cell phones and be present with us." I do as instructed, then grab a white wooden chair in the second row next to Dylan and Evie. A wall of glass windows provides a stunning view of the water. The groomsmen enter from the side, followed by the best man—that's Max—and Chase, the man of the hour. They stand by the glass at the front.

A professional photographer is poised at the entry-way, ready to do his job. A string quartet picks up their bows and plays something that sounds like Beethoven. All eyes turn to the doors. A bridesmaid I don't know comes in first. She might be Lily. The name sounds familiar.

When the first bridesmaid is ten feet down the aisle, Mia enters.

My sister's words ring in my ears.

How would you feel if you never took the chance?

They repeat in my head as I stare. I can't take my eyes off her.

She wears a yellow dress and clutches a bouquet of daisies. Her hair is twisted up, but several caramel-blond strands fall softly around her face. As she walks down the aisle, my heart battles to break out of my chest and run to her.

Those dimples I adore.

Those eyes I want to look into.

Those lips I want to kiss.

As she nears the front, her gaze locks firmly with mine, and I swear I can see her mouth form the barest word. A *hi* just for me.

A few more bridesmaids enter and join the wedding party at the front, but I lose track of who's who and who's here because I can't stop looking at Mia, even when the bride enters to "Ode to Joy."

I try to focus on the ceremony, on the words the offi-ciant says to Chase and an absolutely radiant Josie, who's as beautiful as any bride. He pledges to love her for the rest of his life, and she vows to do the same, and soon platinum bands encircle their fingers, and the groom kisses the bride as claps and cheers erupt throughout the boathouse.

How would I feel?

Like I'd missed the greatest chance of my life.

Mia's the one, no matter how far or how close she is, and I'll tell her as soon as I get her in my arms.

16

In the rom-com movies my sister made me watch growing up—and by *made me*, I mean she baked the most delicious brownies and I was only allowed to eat them if I watched her flicks—the hero runs to the heroine and tells her right away when he realizes precisely how he feels.

In real life, there's a lot of waiting around.

A lot of small talk.

A lot of "how do you know the groom and bride" and "what do you do" conversations with people I'll never talk to again. That's okay. I don't mind. I'm good at small talk, and frankly, it's part of my job. But it occupies an inordinate amount of my evening and makes it damn hard to find a spare moment with the sister of the groom.

Since she's in the wedding party, the photographer whisks the crew away shortly after the ceremony to snap sunset photos of the group. I down a glass of champagne, eat some kind of mushroom appetizer, and chat with friends, family, and random doctors from Chase's hospital. When they learn what I do, they seem particularly interested in sharing stories about some of the most absurd outdoor injuries they've treated, from gnarly broken bones to dangerous wild animal bites. It's like we're on two sides of the equation. I've seen or heard of the mishaps as they occurred, and they've treated them.

"What about you? Ever been injured in the woods?" a doctor with glasses and a crooked nose asks.

"Sure. I've had my share of wounds, from a broken arm to a sprained ankle. But hey, I've never been skunked or bitten by a raccoon, so there's that." I tap a wooden beam for luck. "And I've managed to avoid tripping on twigs."

The guy laughs. "You don't want to end up with a twig in the wrong place."

And I don't want to think about what that place would be, either, so I politely excuse myself.

These random conversations continue throughout the evening, into the reception, and during the dinner itself. At one point, Mia swishes past me, stopping briefly to whisper, "Nice tie."

"Nice everything," I say.

She purses her lips and blows me the barest of kisses.

Then she's gone, chatting with her mother, chatting with her father, talking to Max. I keep myself busy, catching up on the latest from Dylan and his identical twin, Flynn. Honestly, if Dylan weren't holding my sister's hand, I'd be hard-pressed to tell the brothers apart.

The evening unfurls into toasts, laughter, delicious food, buzz-worthy champagne, and more happiness than I've ever seen in one place. Chase and Josie move onto the deck for their first dance as husband and wife, and when "Overjoyed" by Matchbox Twenty ends, they dance through another song, then another, as more guests join in.

One of the groomsmen rises, and for a second, I think he's going to ask Mia to dance. I'm not okay with that. Not in the least.

I stand, cut a path across to her, and hold out my hand. "Dance with me."

Her smile lights up her face. "I was hoping you'd ask."

Out on the dance floor, we join dozens of couples. Mia's parents, Josie's parents, Spencer's parents, and Charlotte's parents, too. Max and Henley laugh as they shimmy, and I faintly remember him mentioning once that Henley loves to salsa and had taken him to dancing lessons. I knew then she was the one for him, hook, line, and sinker. I'd never thought anyone could lure Max to a dance floor. But now he twirls his fiancée in a circle. He doesn't even balk when he sees me take Mia in my arms.

She places her arms on my shoulders, and mine circle her hips, as chastely as I can manage. The lights on the deck twinkle, and the stars wink in the night sky. Tall buildings in Manhattan tower around us, sprinkling their own light in an iridescent nighttime painting.

Mia fiddles with my tie, running her fingers over the knot. "So where's your plus-one?" she asks, staring at the knot.

"I'm hoping she's right here. And you?"

She smiles, the kind of smile she can't seem to contain. "The same might be true for me." Instinctively, I wrap my hands tighter around her hips.

"We fit," she says softly, just for me. The way she looks at me triggers a rush of heat across my skin.

"I'd say we fit incredibly well."

"Do we?"

"We do, Mia." I want to bring her closer, kiss her till she's drunk on me.

"I know." She swallows, waiting for more, it seems.

Good. I want to go first. "I can't stop thinking about you."

"You mean the other night?" she asks, her voice like a feather. "You can't stop thinking about the other night?"

I shake my head. "No. Just you. Everything about you."

A smile tugs at her lips. "Everything?"

"Every single thing," I say, taking my time with each word. "Kissing you. Touching you. Knowing you."

"But there are reasons . . ."

I shake my head and lift her chin. "I don't care about the reasons not to be with you," I say, my voice low but firm, because once you realize you might miss out on the greatest chance ever, the reasons shrink to nothing. "I don't care about the miles. I don't care that we live on different coasts. All I care about is how I feel, not only when I'm near you, but when I think of you. Don't you see how you make me feel?"

"How do I make you feel?"

My gaze drifts down, taking in the view of her in my arms. Her strong, toned body, the lines of her neck, the softness of her skin. I dip my face near her neck, ever so subtly inhaling her. She intoxicates me. "Like my body is humming. Like I'm vibrating. Everything crackles when I'm with you."

I meet her eyes once more. Those eyes—I could get lost in them. Hell, maybe I've already gone missing. Maybe I'll never be found because this is where I want to be.

She draws a deep breath. "There's a lot I want to tell you, Patrick." I tense, my shoulders tightening, my body going rigid. This can't be good. "But when we're like this, I can't really think."

Her breath flutters across my jaw, and it stokes the flames inside me.

"And why's that?"

"Because of how you make me feel," she whispers.

I relax. That's better. Maybe whatever she wants to tell me is something we can deal with. "How do I make you feel?"

"Like I want to be in my body and out of my body," she whispers. Her palm slides up the back of my neck, and I nearly growl. Her back is to the crowd, and we're at the edge of the deck. No one can see that her fingers have traveled into my hair. She plays with the ends, and her touch drives me out of my mind. It's a straight shot of lust to my chest, and heat pools in my groin.

"Mia," I whisper, almost a warning.

Her fingers thread through my hair. She inches closer. Her lips are so damn near to me. "But most of all, I feel like I want you in my body."

I groan. I can't even speak. Can't form words. My brain is a haze. It's a hot, fuzzy, static haze, and my fingertips burn with desire as I dig them into her hips. She's reduced me to nothing but lust, nothing but fire, nothing but heat.

She's rendered me speechless, aroused, and completely, absolutely over the moon.

"Jesus Christ, Mia," I manage to say, a desperate groan under my breath, and I don't care if Max is watching, or Chase, or anyone. But a quick scan tells me they're all in their own worlds, so with my hands on her hips, I yank her closer, letting her feel what she's done to me.

She smiles, a wild, wicked grin.

But this is more than sex. The way I feel for her is so much more. "Listen," I say, before she kills all my brain cells with her words.

"Talk," she gently commands.

"I don't care that you live in California and I live here. I want to be with you. Even if we're long distance, even if it's hard to see each other, I'm absolutely wild about you, Mia," I say, and my heart feels a thousand times lighter.

And then a thousand times fuller when she says, "It's the same for me." Her body melts against mine as if it's as much of a welcome relief for her to speak her truth as it is for me to speak mine. "I thought I would go out of my mind if I didn't say something."

"I wish I could kiss you right now." My eyes survey the crowd, our friends and family dancing on the deck with us. As much as I want to crush my lips to hers, now's not the time for that kind of public display of affection.

"Kiss me tonight, then. Can I come over later? When the wedding ends?"

"If you don't, I think I might die," I say, laughing.

She levels me with her gaze once more. "Don't die until you make love to me."

I'm fried. I'm toasted. I've never wanted anything as much as I want Mia under me, over me, with me all night. "That's all I'll be doing once you knock on the door."

She curls her hand around my shoulder. "There's something else I want to tell you." Her voice is wobbly, and my chest hollows with her words.

But I steel myself to take a hit tonight. Let's do this. Let's finish it. I need to know once and for all what I'm up against.

A shriek of excitement cuts across the deck. "It's finally time for cake!"

We both startle and turn toward Nick's pregnant wife, who's pointing excitedly at the towering white cake as she calls the wedding party over.

Once more, my arms are empty.

17

I flick on the light, unknot my tie, and say hello to Zeus.

He rubs against my leg and meows. I understand immediately. I scoop a handful of his favorite kibble into a bowl, and set it on the floor.

I turn on another light in the living room and contemplate pouring a Scotch. Feels like a night for the amber liquid. The kind of evening where I'll pace around my pad, hoping she'll arrive soon. A night when I should flop on the couch, stare into the distance, and think dark thoughts.

But that's not who I am.

Even if Mia has things to tell me, I can handle them. That's what I do. I handle stuff.

Rather than pace, I grab a book, my dog-eared and well-worn paperback of *A Prayer for Owen Meany*. I flip it open to a random page and read words I've read many times before.

The knock on my door comes quickly, and I open it. Mia strides in with purpose, her chin high, her eyes fierce. She places her hands on my chest, as if she's warding me off. "I told myself I wouldn't do this."

All the air spills out of me. "Why?"

"I dated a good friend of Max's right after college."

And that's the reason. That's all the reasons, it seems. "What happened?"

Her hazel eyes are intense. "It didn't end well."

I furrow my brow. "You mean Max didn't handle it well?"

She shakes her head, the loose little strands of her hair moving with her. "It's not about him. It's about me. I've never wanted to get involved with one of his friends since then. That's why I've had to resist you. That's why I've held back before."

I grit my teeth, then will myself to let go of my frustration. "What happened? Who is this guy?"

"His name is Eric."

I search my files for a friend of Max's by that name. But he's never mentioned an Eric, not even in passing. "I've never heard of him."

Mia lets out a long, sad breath. "That's the issue. They aren't friends anymore."

My shoulders sag, and I get it. I understand at last what I'm up against. This cuts so much deeper than the question of when and where I tell Max I'm mad about his sister. This is about whether she'll even let herself cross a huge hurdle.

But Mia surprises me by wrapping her arms around my neck. Pressing her breasts to my chest. Sliding her body against mine.

"Mia," I say, and this time the warning is real. "You tell me you shouldn't do this, and then you *do this*."

"I told you because I want you to know where I'm coming from." She draws a deep breath. "But I don't want us to stop."

I close my eyes, feeling my body sway as if I've had too much to drink, when all I've had is a glass or two earlier. It's not alcohol, though, that makes me feel this way. It's the uncertainty of opening my heart. But even so, I don't want to resist her. I rope my arms around her waist, bringing her closer, walking backward with her toward the kitchen counter.

"I can't think straight when I'm touching you," I say, my voice rougher than it's ever been.

"I can't, either." Her back hits the counter, and I lift her onto it so we're face-to-face and eye-to-eye.

"So what are we doing?" I don't break my gaze. I don't mince words. I serve it straight up. "I don't want half of you. I don't want a fling with you."

"I don't want that, either. All I know is I don't want to hurt Max."

"And I don't want to hurt you."

"But I'm still here." With a clear voice and fierce eyes, she says, "And I don't know how to stop wanting you."

This woman is breaking me down. I don't even know if I can have her the way I want. But I don't want to let her go, either. That means I need to show her. I need to convince her *we* will be different. That I'm not Eric, even though I know nothing about him.

I bend close and push the strap of her dress over

her shoulder. "I won't hurt you." I kiss her neck, her collarbone. "This won't end badly, Mia. I promise you."

"Patrick . . . you don't know that."

I kiss her shoulder, and she shudders. "I do know that. And I mean it. I'm not that guy." I don't know how to make it more obvious without spelling it out for her. But she's not ready to hear the truth—I won't let it end badly because if I have my way, we won't end. Instead, I clasp her face in my hands and say, "You have to know I will do everything to make this good for you. Every single thing between us will be good."

She trembles and circles her arms tighter around my neck. "It's so good already."

Our eyes lock, and the air between us is charged like a live wire. Electric. Ready to burn.

"Then what do you want, Mia? You know what I want. *You.* I want all of you, and I'll tell Max tomorrow how I feel. But if you think you shouldn't be doing this, then you're right. We shouldn't do this. If you need to leave, I need to be the man who lets you walk away."

She closes her eyes, and when she opens them, they shine with heat, with fire, with an insatiable need I recognize instantly. It's how I feel.

"I'm not going anywhere." Her lips curve up in a grin. "Except to your bed. Right this second."

18

———

Our hands move with furious speed as we reach the bedroom.

She tugs at my loosened tie, tossing it onto the mattress. Her quick fingers make fast work of the buttons on my shirt.

"God, you looked so hot in a suit, it's almost a sin to take it off you," she says, as she makes her way down to the last button. "But I'm willing to commit this wrong."

"I couldn't take my eyes off you all night, from the second you walked into the boathouse," I tell her as I spin her around, unhook the zipper on the dress, then slide it down to her waist. She wears a strapless bra and my God, her back is so fucking sensual, so smooth and soft. I unhook her bra and run my fingers along her spine.

She arches into my touch, and then I press my lips to her neck and kiss a slow, lingering path down her back. She shivers with every single kiss. When I stop, I spin her around again to face me, slide the straps down her arms, and let the dress fall to her waist.

My breath hitches.

"Mia," I say, as I cup her breasts, running my thumbs over her nipples, feeling them tighten under my touch. "You're so beautiful. I'm going to sound like a broken record. But, Jesus. Look at you. I can't believe you're here and I'm touching you."

She runs her hands down my chest. "Don't stop."

We move quickly through the rest of our clothes. She tugs at the zipper on my suit pants as I push down the skirt of her dress, letting the pale-yellow fabric pool on the floor. Everything else comes off in seconds, and then I stare at the stunning woman before me. Her silver belly-button ring glints in the moonlight. I run my thumb over it.

My mouth is dry, and my heart slams against my chest. My pulse rockets. "*You.*" I can't form any more words, so gently, I push her to the bed.

She sinks onto the mattress. I kneel before her and open her legs.

She gasps.

I spread them wider, savoring the sight of her wet pussy. "Need to taste you."

"Please," she moans, leaning back on her palms, her tits pushing up, her back arching, her legs wide for me.

I slide my hands under her thighs and bury my face between them.

And I lick.

And I lick.

And I lick.

She's the most intoxicating thing I've ever tasted—sweet and salty and so fucking wet for me. Her silky sweetness coats my lips, gets on my chin, covers my beard.

I can't get enough of her. My cock throbs, a heavy weight between my legs, aching as I devour her.

Something happens when you touch the person you've fantasized about for months. The person you've longed for. You not only want to fuck her, you want to adore her with every part of you.

Right now, my mouth is going to deliver that message, because that's how I feel—I want to fuck her with my tongue and cherish her with my lips.

I want her to know how badly I want to fuck every part of her, and how much I'll adore her. That's how I taste her. That's how I eat her. The way I want her—every way. I flick my tongue against the delicious rise of her clit, and her hands clamp onto my head, her fingers threading tightly in my hair.

"Ohhhh," she moans, tugging me even closer. I'm not sure I can bury my face any farther into the promised land, but if she needs more of me, I'll give it to her. I'll give her anything she wants.

As I suck hard on her clit, she curls her hands tighter around my skull, then she draws up her legs, so her feet are perched on the edge of the mattress. Like that, she lifts her hips, arching, thrusting, and fucking my face.

I go faster, sweeping my tongue up and down her center, lapping up every last drop of her wetness, then I do it again, since she only gets wetter, flooding my tongue with her desire.

Her scent fills my nostrils, and her pussy is the center of my world. As her noises grow louder, and her cries reach higher, I glide a finger across her. Her gasp is long and feral, and it's a cue to give her more. With two fingers I push inside, and she falls back, her head hitting the bed, her legs widening, and her hands never letting go of my head.

She moans and writhes. "So close."

Come all the fuck over me, I want to tell her, but I won't let go of her pussy. I am a man consumed with the task at hand—making Mia come so hard she forgets any reason she's ever had to back down. Making it so good for her that she knows no one else will ever send her so high.

I move my face back and forth fast, licking and kissing her through her orgasm as she rocks against me like there's no tomorrow. She's moaning and groaning and crying out *so good, so good, so good,* as her body's rhythm slows.

She lets go of her grip, her hands falling to the mattress as she releases a satisfied breath.

I raise my face, wipe a hand over my mouth, and look at my gorgeous woman. She's spent and glowing, and she's still murmuring. I crawl up her body, lower myself to her, letting her feel the weight of my cock against her belly.

Her eyes flutter open. Her smile spreads. Her hazel eyes are glossy. "Hi," she says a little hoarsely, as her hand drifts down to my dick. Her fist curls around me, and I suck in a breath and then groan.

"Hey," I manage to say as she strokes. A shudder racks me as her soft hand explores my shaft, her thumb tracing the head.

"I like this. I like you," she says, all sensual and husky as she wraps her hand tighter.

Her smile fades, and she lets go. My dick misses her hand. A lot.

She pushes up to her elbows. I tense, brace myself for some kind of shift. But instead, she asks me the most wonderful question in the universe. "Can we have sex without a condom? I'm on birth control, and I'm negative. Are you?"

"Fuck yeah, I am," I tell her, and I grip my cock in one hand, settle between her legs, and rub the head against her sweet, hot pussy.

She lifts her hips, seeking me out. Flames lick my skin, and I groan. It's such a rush, such a high. There is nothing like this. Nothing like knowing that my Mia wants the same things as I do right now.

She's ready. She's so damn wet. But I want her begging. I want her needing me. I want her to know from the way I fuck her that I'm not like any other man in her past. I need her to know I'm the one she'll always want.

Gripping my dick, I rub against her, touching her wetness with the head, letting her feel me all over her— up, down, around, then right there, on her most sensitive spot. I rub, and I play, and I work her into a frenzy again.

"So good," she cries out, lifting and rocking and trying desperately to draw me into her body—her body, where she said she wanted me tonight.

"You want me inside you, Mia?" I growl.

"Please, yes," she groans, letting her knees fall wide for me.

I give her just the tip, and it electrifies me. I tremble because it's so damn good. "You want me to bury my cock all the way in you?"

She rocks her hips. "I do. I want you in me."

"You want to feel all of me, baby, or is this enough?" I give her a little bit more. My meaning should be perfectly clear. If Mia wants me, she'd better want everything I have to give.

"I want all of you. I want you to fuck me. I want you."

Kneeling between her legs, I push in another inch. I shudder. "How's this?"

"More," she groans.

"You want it all?"

"Yes," she says, practically bowing her back off the bed. "I want all of you."

I give in, sinking into her, burying my cock inside her, and then lowering myself to her. "You need to know, with me, you can have everything."

She wraps her legs around my lower back. "That's what I want."

I hold nothing back. I fuck her hard. I fuck her slow. I fuck her fast. I fuck her so she knows she's the one. I give her everything I have as I move inside her. As I swivel my hips. As I pump into her.

She moans, and murmurs, and cries my name. Her hair is a wild tangle, strands pressed to her face as she moves with me, her hips lifting and thrusting and rising.

We move as if we're meant to come together. I reach down to her thigh, pushing her right knee up to her chest.

"Gymnastics comes in handy," I say, laughing lightly.

"The other one, too," she says, and pleasure camps out in my whole damn body.

I push her left knee up so they're both hiked to her chest. Then she drapes them over my shoulders. She wiggles her hands between us, sliding them to my face. Gripping my jaw, she lets me do all the work, as she gives herself over to how I fuck her.

"We fit," she says, on a pant.

"So incredibly well," I groan, driving into her. As I pull back, my shaft slides against her clit, and she moans so damn loudly.

"Like that, like that," she pants, and I take her and make love to her until she's so far gone, she's digging her fingers into my jaw as she gasps *oh God, oh God, oh God.*

Then she keens. It's beautiful and primal. The world disappears as Mia comes again, lost in her orgasm, her eyes squeezed shut, her breath ragged, her moans guttural and gorgeous.

There are no more words for me, either. Just grunts and growls.

I pump faster, harder, more furiously until my

vision goes white and the room turns to a neon-hot blur. Pleasure crackles along my spine, surging inside me, barreling down my cock as I empty myself inside her, filling her up.

Then I collapse onto Mia, wrap my arms around her, and whisper in her ear. "I'm not letting you go."

I can feel her smile against me. "It's a good thing I'm not leaving then."

19

I prop myself on my elbow. "I like the sound of you not leaving, but feel free to elaborate."

Her eyes twinkle like she just scored a deal on airline tickets to Paris and can't wait to share the news. "I'm moving to New York."

And the City of Lights can't hold a candle to that one.

I blink.

This can't be happening.

I've fallen into the most vivid, lucid dream of my life.

"Are you screwing with me?"

She shakes her head. Her smile is as wide as the sky, her voice full of joy. "I'm not joking. I'm relocating Pure Beauty to New York. I'm so ridiculously excited about this, and everything was finalized today. Now I can tell you. That's what I was going to tell you before Harper's cake announcement."

"It was?" I figured it was the Eric thing, since that's what she led with when she arrived.

"Yes. But then when I came over here, I had other things I needed you to know, too, and honestly, after that, I wanted to focus on getting you naked."

"Yeah, I'm totally into the whole naked thing, too," I say, admiring her bare skin as she lies next to me. In my bed. If questioned under oath, I'd still have to go with this being a dream. "You're really not messing with me about moving?"

"Apparently, you think I'm a mean trickster, because that would be a cruel joke." She pushes my chest then trails her fingers down my torso, dancing them across the planes of my abs, as if she's only now realized she has permission to touch me whenever she wants.

Does she ever.

But . . .

Removing the distraction, I take her hand and curl my fingers around hers, squeezing. "Are. You. Serious?"

"Yes. The podcast? My epiphany? All the new things going on with my company? It's not a beauty product for cats, obviously. It's that I want to be here in New York."

Zeus jumps up on the bed, as if on cue. He lands on silent paws and pads up the covers, slinking between us. I stroke his back, and he arches into my hand.

Mia scratches his chin. "You're naturally beautiful. You don't need a single product," she says to him.

There goes my heart again. She talks to my cat. "What made you realize you wanted to be in New York? You've always lived on the West Coast."

"Everything." She strokes the beast as he perches imperiously on the pillow and launches into a fastidious face washing. "Being here made me realize what I miss every day – my brothers, and they're both here now, of course. Everyone has moved from the West Coast to New York. Plus, I have great friends in the city, like Dylan and Olivia, and some of my suppliers are here so it makes it easier to do business. My VP of products, Lisa, grew up in Connecticut, so it works for her, too. And when I had dinner with my brothers last weekend, everything crystallized. Josie's now my sister-in-law and I want to get to know her better. Same for Henley soon too. I don't want to be the lone wolf out on the other side of the country while everyone goes about their life. I want to be near my family. My brothers are the two people I'm closest to, and I miss them more every day. They might even be having kids soon."

I raise an eyebrow. "Does that mean Chase needed to get Josie down the aisle, stat?"

Mia laughs, shaking her head. "No. At least, I don't think so. But Max will be married in a few months, and I have no doubt they'll all be having kids in the near future. I want to see them regularly. I want to see any nieces and nephews I might have regularly, too. I feel so good about this decision."

So do I.

Though, I'd feel a bit better if she happened to include in her list of reasons a certain guy she just banged. The one thing she hasn't mentioned is me. I keep it light and playful when I say, "And Zeus was obviously a big factor, since you can't keep your hands off him."

"He's irresistible." Then she covers his ears and stage whispers, "He knew about it all along. I told him earlier in the week that it might happen."

I stare at my cat as he licks a white paw, then rubs it against his cheek. "I seriously can't believe you kept this from me, Zeus."

"He's a shrink. He keeps all my secrets. I think it's like patient–pussycat privilege."

"He is something of a vault." Time to stop dicking around. *Just ask her directly if I even made it to the pros and cons list.* "Are you doing this at all because of us?"

She swallows, and her eyes widen. The look in them reminds me of a teen caught dipping her hand in her mom's wallet. "Because of us?" she squeaks, her voice high.

"Is that outrageous to even ask?" I run a hand down her bare arm, since I sure as hell enjoy having permission to touch her. "I recall a whole conversation earlier tonight about not being able to stop thinking about each other."

She taps my nose with her finger. "Don't worry, Kangaroo. It's not as if I expect you to ask me to move in and marry you."

My lips open, but no sound comes. Her answer throws me. Because honestly, there's a part of me that likes that idea—move in and marry. Maybe not today, maybe not tomorrow, but a lot sooner than later.

Except, she might not be in this to the same degree that I am.

Possibly because of Eric.

Maybe because of Max.

More likely because of her.

And you know what? Even if she isn't all in yet, I'll need to be okay with that. I've wanted Mia for a long time, and now I'll have the chance every goddamn day to convince her how good we can be together. Judging from the length and intensity of the orgasms she's already had, I'm winning her over easily in that department.

Time to play to my strengths.

I move her on top of me, her legs straddling my stomach. "Bring those sweet, gorgeous lips to mine. If you're going to be living here, you need to start practicing your favorite form of arithmetic. I believe on the hike you said it was multiplication."

"I do need to catch up on my math." She leans forward, her tits brushing my chest as she kisses me. I groan at the feel of her lips. I curl a hand through her hair, kissing her deeper, savoring the exquisite taste of her mouth. Her tongue darts between my lips, and we both moan at the same time.

The kiss unfurls like a slow wave rolling toward the shore, one crest spreading into the next as I spend some time with those lips I love.

But soon enough, I stop the kiss. "Let me show you what two times two every single night feels like."

Grasping her hips, I slide her down my body. My dick is doing an excellent full-on salute, and I make sure she gets a proper greeting when I bring her to me.

I draw a sharp breath as she lowers herself onto my erection.

"You feel so incredibly good," she murmurs. Then she moves on me, slow and sensual, taking me in, and then nearly letting me go.

God, it's so good with her. It's mind-blowing. It's astonishing. Sharp, hot pleasure sparks through my body. I watch her every move as her tight figure rises and lowers. She grinds on me, taking me deeper, then picking up speed, sliding her hot wetness up and down. Her tits bounce, her hair swings, her nails dig into my chest.

When she closes her eyes, she leans her head back, and her neck looks so long and inviting. I thrust my hips up, fucking her as she fucks me. Her sounds grow louder, her pants wilder and more erratic. She cries out that she's coming, and it's filthy and sensual at the same damn time as her mouth parts in a perfect *O*. She shudders as she climaxes, and then she crashes onto my chest, murmuring as she threads her hands in my hair, "I need one more to make it four."

"Let's do it," I say. I pull out, flip her to her hands and knees, and bury myself in her again. What a gorgeous sight to see Mia bent over for me in the middle of my bed, offering her body and letting me take her. I band an arm around her waist, slide my hand between her legs, and work her clit until she comes once more on my cock.

And as she pants and moans, I don't have to hold back anymore. It's my turn, and I unleash several fast, hard pumps, as pleasure rockets through me. I join her on the other side, my own orgasm pulsing hard through me, coming as I groan her name.

After we clean up, I gather her in my arms. "I like that last position," Mia murmurs as she nestles against my chest.

"I like all positions with you."

She laughs. "Yes, I do so far, too. But I *really* like that one."

"You mean *doggy style*, Mia?" I say, since she can't seem to say it. "And I thought you were an animal lover."

"Yes, Patrick. I like it doggy style." She swats my hip. "And you're a dog."

"I'll take that as a compliment." I stare at the ceiling for a moment, thinking back on how fantastic this night has been, even if she's not as full speed ahead as I am yet. "Hey, do you think when dogs do it, they call it doggy style?"

She shakes her head. "No. It's just *style* then."

"Then, we have a lot of styling to do once you move to New York."

She wedges herself even closer to me, and I thank my lucky stars she's a top-notch snuggler. "Like, maybe every night styling."

I kiss her hair, both satisfied that she's with me now and even more determined to prove to her that moving to this city will be the best thing she's ever done.

20

Conversations with the Cat
Zeus

The sun shone brightly through the window as the woman engaged in one of Zeus's favorite activities—rubbing his belly. He demonstrated his appreciation by lounging on his back and stretching his legs as far as he could.

Supercat.

The elegant, seductive pose showed off how long and lean his body was. This way she could admire his belly, too. It was quite a handsome stomach by any mammalian standard, sleek and covered in the softest fur.

"Did you hear the news? I'll be seeing you more often," the woman said.

The man wasn't here. He'd left a few minutes ago,

pulling on some clothes and grabbing his keys after patting the woman's rumbling tummy.

"I still have lots of details to work out, and I need to find a place to live. Or I could just move in with you," she said then laughed. "Shh. Don't tell Patrick I said that. I'm sure he'd think it's too soon. I suspect he thought I was only moving for him, and it freaked him out last night."

Zeus twitched his tail, yet another incredibly lovely feature that he possessed. Such a good-looking tail.

"I'm doing this because it makes sense for me. I'll find my own place easily. I don't want to scare him away, especially since I'm already crossing a line I swore I'd never cross after what happened with Eric. But it's different with Patrick, you know what I mean? So different. I can't see it playing out the same way this time since I feel so much more for him." Sighing, she flipped onto her back. "And obviously I want to see him more. Of course, he's part of why I'm moving. I'd love to see him as much as possible. But who knows if he's even thinking along those lines. . ." her voice drifted off and turned into a long sigh. "Sometimes your mind goes to these places when you're madly in love with someone and have been for months." She turned to stare at him. "You know what I'm talking about? Of course you do, you sly fox. I've seen the way you look at that calico."

He answered her with a deep, rumbling purr. He liked to think he understood humans as perfectly as any feline ever had.

21

The clock keeps ticking closer to Mia's flight back to the West Coast tonight. She won't return to New York for a month, she said, since she has business to attend to in San Francisco, prepping for her relocation. I won't be counting the days till she returns.

The thirty-four days, that is. Fine, the thirty-four days and six hours.

Max and Henley stayed at a hotel last night, so after I make sure my hungry Mia eats breakfast, she heads upstairs to his apartment to tackle work for the day. I leave for a run and a bike ride, then I upload some of Zeus's shots from a recent hike to his Instagram account and respond to a ton of replies the popular fur ball received in the last few days.

Later, Max texts to invite me to an impromptu dinner. Chase and Josie leave for their honeymoon tomorrow, and he's having them over before they go. Since it's no longer technically Chase's day, that makes tonight the night to tell Max.

I head upstairs with a bottle of wine and join my buddy, his fiancée, the newlyweds, Henley's best friend, Olivia, and the woman I screwed senseless last night to the tune of four orgasms, with two more this morning.

Yes, folks, I'm sending her to San Francisco with a half dozen orgasms in less than twenty-four hours to remember me by. I'd say that's a good showing. I'll need to pull off a victory in the all-around, too, but I'm awarding myself a gold medal in Making Mia Meow.

At dinner, Henley serves her now-famous home-made mac and cheese as we recap the best and goofiest moments from the wedding. As Olivia recounts Harper's cake shout-out, I catch Mia's eye, and the second I do, she blushes. I can't help but smile because I love that all it takes to turn her cheeks rosy is one knowing look. I wiggle an eyebrow as I drink the wine. She nibbles on the corner of her lip then casts her eyes down.

"Just a heads-up. I do plan to scream when it's cake time at your wedding, too," Josie says to Max and Henley, prompting Henley to show off her ring.

"Speaking of our wedding, check out my ring for the thirtieth time."

"It's like looking at the sun," Olivia declares.

Henley glances from her ring to Josie's. "The Summers men do have most excellent taste."

Mia clears her throat. "Ahem. Where do you think they learned how to pick out rings?"

I laugh and raise a glass. "To the happy couple, and the secret weapon of a sister who helped choose the most beautiful diamonds for both her brothers."

When dinner is over, Max and Henley clean up, shooing us to the pool table. After a quick round, Chase and Josie take off, and Olivia leaves, too. The hosts join us at the table as Mia peers at the time on the wall. "I better make sure I have everything for my flight."

"I'll help you check," Henley says, and the women head to the guest room. A few seconds later, they're listening to the Go-Go's as Mia packs.

I take a deep, fueling breath. As Max grabs a stick and Belinda Carlisle gives us some privacy, I say what I've wanted to say for months.

"This seems as good a time as any to let you know something that's been on my mind."

Max stares as he lines up his shot. "You want me to fix your car for free?" He heaves an over-the-top sigh. "Fine, if I must. But I insist on you hooking me up with your dealer for that kick-ass ride of yours. I need one of Carlos's custom-made bikes."

I smile. "Consider it done." Then I clear my throat. "What I wanted to say, though, is I'm falling in love with your sister."

His spine straightens, and he blinks. "Excuse me?"

"I think you understood me." I smile.

"You're in love with my sister?"

There's no question in my mind. That's where I am on the map with Mia. I'm falling headfirst and fast. "It was pretty instant when I met her here several months ago. We've had a connection from day one."

He draws a deep breath. "You two have always gotten along," Max concedes. "Are you guys together now?"

"It only started last night for real. I wanted to let you know as soon as I had a chance, and today seemed the best time, now that the wedding is over."

He nods slowly. Rubbing a hand across the back of his neck, he says, "I appreciate you telling me."

"And listen, you know I'll be good to her. I'll treat her so damn well."

"I have no doubt."

"And since she's moving to New York, we're going to make a real go of it."

"And she's down with this?" He sounds skeptical. Way more skeptical than I thought he'd be.

"Yeah. She is."

"Are you sure?"

I scoff. "I know the score, and I get it."

"Okay, then." He resumes his pace around the table, looking for the right shot. But something about the turn this conversation has taken bugs me.

"I'm not going to be like that other guy. I'm not going to hurt her, so you don't have to worry."

Max scratches his jaw. "It's not her I worry about, buddy." He claps my shoulder and pins me with his dark gaze. "It's you."

Tension bolts through me. "What does that mean?"

Max tips his forehead to the kitchen. "When Henley and I were cleaning up, she said she thought you had it bad for Mia, and it seems you do. In my humble opinion, when a man feels that way about a woman, he opens himself up for a world of hurt if it goes south."

It won't go south, I want to say. It's all looking up. I keep my mouth shut, though, as Max continues.

"I have no doubt you'll be good to her. Hell, I'm sure you'll be great to her. But Eric was good to her, too. Trouble was, she wasn't in love with him, and he didn't get over her when they broke up. That's why we're not friends."

With brutal clarity, I understand what I'm up against. When Mia said she feared this not ending well, it was a warning. She might not feel the same way I do.

On the drive to the airport, I do my best to put the conversation with Max out of my mind. No need for baggage, right?

The past is the past.

The present is a gift.

I'm not the dude who dwells on what went wrong. I focus on the here and now. On Mia and me. On what I can offer her. *Normal, considerate, easygoing.* That's my stock-in-trade, and I aim to deliver.

I keep the conversation free and easy. We chat about the new product lines she's working on, as well as the volunteer work she hopes to do with animal rescues here in New York.

"WildCare is my jam," she says, drumming her fingers on the dashboard. "I need to hook up with something like that in Manhattan."

"I've no doubt we can find an organization like that for you," I say, turning into the airport parking lot.

Mia smiles. "*We*. You said we."

I raise an eyebrow as I search for a spot. "Any reason I shouldn't say we?"

She shakes her head. "No. I just like that you think of us as a we."

Okay, then. Score one for this guy on Project Make Mia Fall Madly in Love with Me.

"And I'll be hoping the next thirty-four days pass quickly," she adds.

I breathe another small sigh of relief. Yep, I'm going to stay the course. Build on this connection the two of us have. That's how I'll deal with the Eric issue. I'll make sure Max and I stay friends, because our friendship matters to me, and because I don't intend to lose his sister. My goal is to keep winning Mia's heart every goddamn day.

And her body, too.

And her tummy, since I know that's a key route to her ticker.

"You'll be back in New York before we know it." Then I remember a booking Dana told me about in our meeting—a trip she wanted me to handle in California. Maybe, just maybe, I can squeeze in a visit with Mia while I'm there. Nothing like a little proximity to make Mia remember why I'm the guy she can't stop thinking about. "You know, I think I have a trip on the West Coast in the next few weeks. Something in Tahoe. I don't have all the details yet."

"How serendipitous," she says, a playful glint in her eyes, as I pull into a parking spot. "Maybe we can have lunch."

"Yeah, let's do lunch, Mia," I say drily, since we both know we want more than lunch.

I cut the engine, open her door, and take her bag. "Carry-on?"

She scoffs. "As if there's any other way to fly."

"Traveling light. I love it."

As we head inside, she checks her phone. "Oh!" Her eyebrows rise in excitement.

"Let me guess. Your flight was canceled, and you're excited about the extra half dozen orgasms I can give you tonight?"

As travelers scurry past us, and announcements boom in the terminal, Mia stops in her tracks and tap dances her fingers down my shirt. "Or maybe the half dozen orgasms you can give me in a tent."

My interest perks up, as well as my dick. I loop my arm around her waist and yank her against me.

"Well, hello there, hard wood," Mia says in a purr.

I laugh. "Speaking of wood, and hard wood, and woods, I *would* very much like to get you under me in a tent." I lower my voice. "And in your favorite position, too. On your hands and knees."

She shivers against me. "Maybe on a little secluded trail somewhere?"

"I'm liking the sound of this in-the-woods seduction. You, me, a campfire, and a sleeping bag to share. Is that what you're thinking? Because I would love to make you come under the stars."

She hums her yes out loud, and then she kisses my jaw.

Proximity—it's exactly what we need to make sure

we work. We need to see each other. We need to touch each other. I need to remind her why she's breaking her rule for me.

She pulls back and meets my eyes. "I'm thinking I'd like to melt marshmallows with you in, say, another week or two when you lead the corporate retreat we just hired you for."

My world goes deafeningly silent amidst all the beeps and buzzes of the noisy terminal, the boarding-soon calls, and the baggage announcements.

They are a wasteland of sound to my ears.

"What?" I somehow manage to say, setting my hands on her shoulders.

"That California client you have? I was hoping you'd be the one handling the trip because that's me! That's Pure Beauty. We don't have to wait thirty-four days to see each other," she says, bouncing up and down, radiating pure glee. "Surprise!"

"The Tahoe client is you?" I ask, dumfounded.

"Yes! You convinced me."

"I convinced you?" I ask, and now I'm doubly dumbfounded.

"You told me how great the rafting trip was for the company that merged. And I thought since I'm moving my employees, this could be a great bonding experience for those making the transition, and it's something we can keep doing once we're all in New York. To make us a better team. Help us navigate the change. Isn't that what you specialize in with the corporate retreats?"

"Yeah," I say, a stone lodged in my chest. I scrub a hand across my jaw.

"I'm sorry," she says, bringing her hand to her mouth. "Is this too soon? Is this a bad surprise? I thought it would be great for all of us. And I just received the confirmation from Felicia, who set it up. She said she was talking to Dana at your company. That was what I was so excited about when I looked at my phone."

Mia shows me an email from Dana confirming that *our CEO and founder will be perfect for your Tahoe trip and the ongoing monthly adventure tours when your move to New York is complete. Can't wait for you to meet Patrick Milligan. He's a total pro outdoors, with years of experience, and all our clients love him.*

Awareness hits me hard. Dana never gave me the names of the new clients when we last met. We don't usually discuss them as we plot out which guides will handle which bookings. We assign trips based on skill level, as well as the type of retreat. When Dana gave me the basic details—a small company wanting to contract ongoing trips to foster an ideal transition to a new location—she said I'd be perfect for it.

And I'd agreed.

And that also means I'm going to California to see Mia in a couple weeks. Which is precisely against the corporate guidelines I signed off on.

"Mia, we can't be involved if I'm working for you. I have a strict rule for all employees, including myself."

Her jaw drops. "What?"

"I had some trouble earlier this year," I say, explaining the issues that led me to tighten the rules. I give a half-hearted grin. "You could just fire us."

Her sigh is heavy. "Felicia already transferred the funds for the deposit."

23

For a moment—okay, a few long moments—this feels insurmountable.

But am I a man or am I a man? I guide people across the toughest trails, up mountains, and over rapids, for crying out loud.

If I can't find my own way across this swamp of a situation, then I should fire myself, and that's not what I'm going to do. When you're in the woods, you solve problems. Hell, if I can start a fire with a battery and clean a mess kit with dirt, then I can sure as hell tackle this problem head-on.

"Don't worry. I know what to do," I say, then I tell Mia my plan.

She shrugs and shoots me a lopsided smile. "And that's why you're not a douchey marsupial."

I grab her face, kiss her hard in front of the Sunday night crowds heading to distant lands, and watch as she makes her way quickly through the TSA PreCheck line.

She waves from the other side of security, and then she's gone.

I head to my car, ready to tackle this new twist. Sure, it would be a hell of a lot easier to win her whole heart if I could use all the tools in the tool kit. I'd like to have my dick play its very capable part at making Mia happy.

Instead, I psych myself up for back-to-basics time with her.

* * *

In a hotel's rooftop garden in Gramercy Park a few days later, Evie gives me a sharp-eyed stare. "Why don't you just assign her a new guide?"

"Obviously, that thought has occurred to me," I say, since that's the first thing I considered.

"Then why didn't you do it?" Evie asks as she wanders through the exclusive establishment, a ten-table garden restaurant that she considers perfect for a first date. I follow her as she tests each table, like Goldilocks, for one of her potential couples. The restaurant is empty since it's midday, but the manager is letting her check it out.

"Because I can handle it," I say. She pats the seat across from her, and I take it. "Besides, she requested me. And yes, I have guides, and I will still have a local guide along with me, but this is my specialty, leading this type of adventure tour-slash-retreat. This is why she hired *my* company." I tap my chest for emphasis. "For me."

Evie rises and gestures to the next table. "Fine. No one is as good as you. I understand."

"That's not what I mean. But it also is what I mean. If someone hires you as a matchmaker, they want you. They want Evie Milligan, the matchmaker who searches for the optimal table in a rooftop garden restaurant to make sure her potential match has the best first date possible."

She turns and stares at me. "But if I had junior matchmakers, I'd farm out some of the work."

"Would you, though?" I ask pointedly as she tries a table in the far-right corner with a stunning view of downtown Manhattan. "Or would you still test all the tables yourself?"

She narrows her eyes and wags a finger. "Fine, fine. I understand. It's not one you can hand off. Why not just change the rules, though?"

I slash a hand through the air. "No way. We revised the employee guidelines for a reason. I can't just say, 'Oh, I was kidding.' And I definitely can't say they don't apply to me."

"But isn't she your girlfriend now? That doesn't make her exempt?"

"Oddly enough, I didn't make a girlfriend provision." I smack my forehead. "What was I thinking?" Evie rises, and I follow her to one more table. "But seriously, if I use that loophole, then anyone can give retroactive relationship-status to whoever they hook up with. No screwing the customers has to mean no screwing the customers."

She runs her hand along the crisp tablecloth. "Is

there that much boinking in the woods that you need these hardcore rules?"

I laugh. "Have you ever been camping? I swear half the babies in the world have been made in tents. It's one huge bang-fest sometimes."

"I guess that's why you went into this field," she says playfully.

"Ha ha. But seriously, it's all good. I have a plan."

She sits in the chair, crossing her legs. "And what is this brilliant plan?"

I sit across from her and lay out my strategy. "I'll do her trip, as requested, as planned. But I'll also spend some time beforehand finding the best guide for her here on the East Coast, so I can reassign her company when she moves to New York. I have enough people out here who can handle the type of day trips she wants once she's here, so I just need to work with Dana and find the right match. And as for the Tahoe trip, I'm the guy. I'm the one who needs to lead it," I say, cracking my knuckles. "And that means I'll be a good Boy Scout."

Evie doubles over. "That's a good one."

"Why is that so funny?"

She points at me. "You think"—she's laughing so hard she can barely breathe—"that you"—more laughter bursts from her—"can put the genie back in the bottle?"

I square my shoulders. "Easy as pie."

After all, what's so hard about a week of celibacy with the woman I'm obsessed with?

24

Day One is a piece of cake. After we ride around the Truckee River on mountain bikes in the morning, Mia and her twenty-five employees take a break to play the stuck-on-a-deserted-island game, a standard icebreaker for these sorts of retreats.

"Which three items would you want if you were stranded on a deserted island?" Mia asks from her perch on a large boulder at the edge of the water, rays of sunlight stretching across the blue surface behind her.

She looks to Lisa, her VP, who I've learned is the practical one, which she demonstrates when she picks a map, a knife, and a satellite phone.

"I like that. I'll stick by your side," Mia says.

Next is a guy named Otis who works in the IT department. He opts for swim trunks, sunscreen, and a Tardis, thrusting a fist in the air rocker-style as he shouts, "TV is educational. Thank you, *Doctor Who*."

Mia nods her appreciation for his answer. "You've always been a master at finding work-arounds."

We go through the rest of the crew, and when it's Mia's turn, she taps her finger against her lip. "I choose a plane, a pilot, and . . . some fuel."

I shoot her a smile that says *well played*.

"And you, Patrick?" Lisa asks, peering over her sunglasses, her black hair in a high ponytail. "It's only fair that the guides play, too." She gestures to me and Blair, a guide I hired recently. Blair pretty much lives and breathes the outdoors. Twin braids run down her back, freckles line her cheeks, and she's always smiling. She'll be with us for the whole trip since the group is large enough to need two guides.

"You want to go first, Blair?"

She shakes her head, her braids swinging. "No way. I'm dying to know what the boss would take."

"Yes, tell us," Otis says, rubbing his palms together, goading me on.

I glance at Mia, who wears a playful *we're waiting* look.

I blow out a long stream of air, stare off into the bright, blue sky, and pretend I'm noodling on the question. "A toothbrush for sure. Since who wants stinky breath when you're stuck, right?"

Lisa narrows her eyes, as if I can't really have given *that* answer.

"A snack would be good," I add, furrowing my brow as if I'm deeply pondering the question. "Maybe an energy bar or a bag of nuts."

"That's what you'd take? A bag of nuts?" an incredulous Otis asks, his eyes bugging out like a cartoon character.

I hold up a finger. "I didn't get to my third item yet." I wiggle an eyebrow. "I'd also take Mia . . . because she has a plane, pilot, and fuel with her."

Otis hoots. "I bow down to you. That's the best work-around ever."

Mia laughs. "And I see Patrick is excellent not only at backpacking, but piggybacking."

When the break ends, just before we hop on our bikes, Mia whispers to me in a flirty voice, "Piggyback-ing," as if it's some new naughty term. Then she stops herself. "Wait. I'm sure that's a terribly inappropriate term for something I don't even want to know about."

I laugh. "Hey now. You're supposed to behave."

We cruise around the lake for the rest of the day, until we return to the inn where everyone is staying for the first two nights of the four-night trip. After dinner and some relaxation time, I call it a night.

Alone.

In my room.

I'll admit it. A part of me hopes Mia will tiptoe over to visit me here on the other side of the inn.

Okay, two parts of me. My dick and my heart.

And fine, my brain wants it, too.

But we made a deal.

Or really, I insisted upon one, and I'm glad she's honoring my wishes, especially when curiosity wins, and I learn the *terribly inappropriate term* refers to when one person piggybacks off another's porn during a solo ride, watching over the shoulder. The way I see it, I don't want to be sneaking up on Mia when she's savoring her own delicious body. I want to be a major player in all the action when she's in my bed, in my home, living in my house.

It's a sharp moment of clarity brought to me by Urban Dictionary.

And I groan with the stark realization that I do want her to live with me. There isn't just a part of me that wants that, like I thought when we joked about it at my apartment. All of me wants that. I don't want to mess around with separate places. I want to pick her up at the airport when she lands in New York in twenty-four more days, and take her to her new home.

Mine.

* * *

Kayak time is the next morning, and Blair leads this part of the trip, while I help her out. After a few hours, the group breaks for lunch. As everyone else heads to picnic tables, Mia hangs back, waiting for me.

"So . . ." A curious tone threads through her voice.

"*So* to you, too."

"Blair's cute."

I glance at Blair, several yards ahead, then to Mia by my side. "Is she?"

"You know she is."

I arch a skeptical brow. "Do I?"

"You do know that."

"I know nothing of the sort." Except that I like Mia's jealousy.

She narrows her eyes and whispers under her breath. "Do you think she's cute?"

I sigh. "Mia, she works for me."

"Do you?" she presses.

I flash her a grin. "Does it drive you up the wall not knowing?"

Her eyes are fierce as she answers, "Yes."

"Why?"

"Because."

"Say it, Mia."

She crosses her arms and huffs.

I shrug as we walk toward the tables. "Okay, don't say it."

"I don't want you to think anyone else is cute," she blurts under her breath.

That's another plus in the quest to win her whole heart—a jealous, possessive Mia. I like her jealous side a hell of a lot. Naturally, I have no choice but to tease her as we amble by the water. A chipmunk scurries along the ground, and I gesture to the little fella. "What about a chipmunk, though? Chipmunks are cute."

"They are."

"How about baby birds? The kind you rescue."

"Stop it. You know I think baby birds are adorable, and you're clearly allowed to think they're cute, too."

"And what about foxes? Like your foxy ink?"

"Foxes are the cutest things ever."

I stop, cross my arms, and peer over my shades. In a voice for her ears only, I give her what she wants at last. "Jackrabbit, I only have eyes for you."

Even though we're side by side, gazing at the water, I can tell her grin is spreading far and wide.

The second night is tougher.

But my copy of *A River Runs Through It*—the book, not the Brad Pitt flick—keeps me occupied, as does a few hours of work, checking in with Dana on the other tours underway, and touching base with clients and suppliers. Before I'm ready to hit the hay, Daisy sends me a picture of Zeus rubbing his cheek against the pot of catnip, captioned: *It's high time you gave him the herb!*

I laugh, then because I'm sure Mia would love to see this, I leave my room and find her curled up on a chair in the living room of the inn, reading a *National Geographic* piece on Arctic exploration. I grab the chair across from her and show her the screen. "He likes your gift."

She sets down the magazine. "Please have him make a list of his likes and dislikes so I can continue to bestow only the finest presents upon him when I'm living in New York."

Mia in New York. Those words sound foreign. The idea of her living in the same city as me feels strange and almost unreal. Maybe because we're riding this in-between state right now, trying to balance all these other complications—her move, my friendship with her brother, and then the most inconvenient hurdle of all—the current can't-touch-this situation.

I'd really like to touch her, just to reconnect. Her knee. Her shoulder. Her hair. I'm a starving man, and any morsel will do.

"Zeus looks forward to your generosity." That feels

even more surreal, as if I'm talking to her through my cat who's not even here. *What I really want to say is I look forward to showering you with affection every single day. And then you'll tell me how much you can't wait for that, too.*

Why the fuck don't I say that? Maybe because Max's warning threw me off. And maybe I'm giving it too much power. But I don't know Mia's whole heart yet, either. She hasn't shared it with me. The last thing I want is to scare her off. I want to nurture this burgeoning thing between us, give it every chance to become all I want it to be. That's why I've kept my mouth shut. After all, one small bout of jealousy is hardly her asking me if she can move in. We're not entirely on the same page here.

Mia cocks her head to the side. "Do you miss him when you travel? Zeus?"

I flip over my phone and check out the shot of the little dude once more. "I do miss him." I hold her gaze. "What about you?"

She licks her lips, her eyes locked with mine, her voice low and soft. "I do miss him. I miss him a lot."

We're not entirely talking about the cat.

But I'm not entirely sure what we're saying, either.

That's the problem.

I want us both to say the same things, to feel the same emotions, and to want this great, big love I believe we can have. And someone is going to need to step it up and speak first.

But if I say all that now, it hardly seems like I'm following my own guidelines. And if we're trying to put the genie back in the bottle, now's not the time for nookie—or for declarations of *I need you with me always*.

The next day the backpacking begins, and I lead the Pure Beauty crew over the hills and through the woods, stopping to snap photos and to breathe in the views—peaks, valleys, and toweringly tall green trees. In the afternoon, we arrive at the campsite, and I work with Blair to set up the tents for the first of two nights in the great outdoors.

A little later around the campfire, Mia runs through more of her team-building and bonding games, including an impromptu round of "What's your special talent?" Mia shows off her party trick, a walking handstand that easily lasts twenty feet. I crack up since it looks like her hands and arms work as upside-down feet and legs. I get a chance to show off mine, too. Making the most kick-ass s'mores ever. Blair helps me with the marshmallows, and for a moment I wonder if Mia's jealousy will return, but she seems focused on her job.

Which I admire.

Selfishly, though, I wish she'd turn her focus elsewhere.

But when it's dark and quiet, and only the owls are hooting and the crickets are chirping, she does just that.

25

Her silhouette frames the flap of the tent as she unzips it, glances behind her, and whispers, "Coast is clear."

I smile at the sight of her sneaking into my tent at midnight. This is a fantasy come to life.

But I silently curse my reality. I can't get any closer to her. That's too risky. Too tempting. I don't stop her, though, from crawling into my tent. Surely I can be near her without kissing her senseless and sliding her under me.

Mia sits cross-legged, her dimples peeking at me briefly.

"Hi," she whispers, taking me back instantly to her *hi* the night we were first together in my bed.

"Hey." I shift in my sleeping bag, propping myself on my elbow.

"I shouldn't be here," she says softly, her lips curving in a guilty grin.

"You shouldn't be here," I echo.

She looks at the tent flap, zipped down. "I don't want to go."

"I don't want you to go."

"Therein lies the dilemma," she murmurs. She takes a deep breath. "Should I go?"

"You should . . ." I inch my hand closer to her.

She glances down at my wandering fingers. "I don't want to tempt . . ."

Heat rushes over my skin. "Tempt you or me?"

She swallows. "Either one of us."

I draw a deep breath. "Guess there's nothing wrong with us just talking, right?"

She shakes her head. "Nothing at all."

I reach her leg and run my fingers across her shin where her yoga pants stop. Her lips fall open in a gasp, and her hand flies to her mouth, covering her sound. A grin plays on my lips. I love that the slightest touch from me turns her on.

"How are you?" I ask.

"I'm turned on now, and it's all your fault."

My fingers travel higher to her knee.

She bites her lip and scoots closer. I brush my fingertips over her thigh, and she closes her eyes, her lips parting as a soft sigh of pleasure falls from them.

"You shouldn't be here," I whisper again.

"I shouldn't be here," she says, as if she's in a trance.

My fingers roam up her legs, and I register every move she makes. The way her knees subtly open wider. How she stretches her neck. The way her hair falls against her skin. How her back arches, as a shudder runs through her whole body when my hand reaches hers and I take it in mine.

"Why are you here then?" I ask, craving her answer. It's torture, absolute torture being this close to her. But I welcome it because even some of Mia is worth the torment.

Her breath is ragged. Her eyes flutter open. She leans closer, bringing her face nearer to mine. "You're hard to resist," she says, and her admission spreads warmth all through me.

"I like knowing it's hard for you, too." My fingers continue their journey, reaching her hip. "Why do you have a fox tattoo? I never asked you before."

She smiles. "A fox was the first animal I rescued in the wild."

"Yeah?"

"When I was nine, I found a little kit in the woods near my home. My parents were working, so Max helped me bring it safely to the house, and he called WildCare while Chase tended to it."

I laugh softly. "Dr. Chase's beginnings as a foxy doctor, revealed on the ten p.m. news."

"The truth comes out."

"That's why you volunteer at WildCare."

"That's why I do what I do at Pure Beauty," she says with passion. "I love animals, and I've wanted to help them my whole life. I don't want to hurt them; I don't want to test on them. That's why I started this company, because I love pretty scents and smells and lotions and potions, and I want to show that it's possible to have everything coexist."

I squeeze her thigh. "I love that you feel that way. It's a gift to do what you love."

"Didn't your favorite writer say, *Do what you love. Know your own bone; gnaw at it, bury it, unearth it, and gnaw it still?*"

"Been studying up on Thoreau's best quotes?"

"Maybe I have. I believe that, too, though. That's why I want to do right by Pure Beauty." She tips her head to indicate the others in their tents, and nervousness flicks across her eyes. "I want them to enjoy working with me. And I hope they're having a good time, but also learning and growing."

"They are," I assure her.

"Thank you for doing such an amazing job, Patrick. These few days have been incredible so far."

"I'm glad you feel that way. And that's also why I won't pull you into my sleeping bag right now. I love what I do, too. I want to do right by my people, as well."

"You are doing right by them." She lays her hand on my sleeping bag, finding and then pressing my hip. "And by me."

I stifle a groan as she repays me by traveling across my hipbone to my leg, and then to the outline of my erection.

I grab her hand, stopping her. "I can't."

She swallows and nods. "I know. I'm sorry,"

"Don't be sorry," I whisper. "Just come back when it's over."

She leans near me, her hair framing her face, tickling my cheeks. "Good night, Patrick," she whispers, then she backs out of the tent, zipping it closed.

She's gone, and there's a part of me that thinks she won't come back. There's a dark part of my heart that fears this surreal sliver of time is all I'll ever have with her. That we won't ever be on the same page. What if Max was right to worry about me meeting the same fate as that other guy?

The guy she didn't love enough.

I should be happy with her unexpected midnight visit. Instead, I'm left not only with an annoying erection, but also with this persistent ache for her in my heart.

Good night, Patrick.

I love you, Mia.

That's what I want to say.

That's what I want to tell her.

I park my hands under my head and stare at the roof of my tent, wishing I could ask her if we're on the same page, if she'll come back when this is over. Instead, I'm searching for the answer in a night sky I can't even see.

But there are no stars to guide me.

In the morning, I rise before everyone else, as the early blue light of dawn begins painting the horizon. I survey the campsite, the orange and green and yellow tents dotting the ground.

I take a deep breath, turn, and walk away from the clearing, along a trail I know well. I have always found answers in the outdoors. Trees have never led me astray, and sunrises have constantly anchored me. The earth has always been honest. I flash back to the moments in my life when I felt the same weight in my chest, a heavy unknown ache.

Where to go to college.

What to study.

Whether to pursue a safe, comfortable career in an office or to take a chance at building a business doing what I love.

Now I need another answer. I need to know if it's time to go all in one more time. To bet everything.

The trouble is, ever since Max told me about Eric, I've been determined to prove I'm different from a guy I know nothing about.

My focus has been all wrong.

As I walk along the trail, the lightening sky keeping me company, I think of Mia, and all the times we've shared. I think of our nights, our days, our moments. I've been so caught up in whether they'll become more than that, that I'm not sure I've seen them completely for what they are.

My perfect days.

I remember the time I took Mia and Zeus for a hike near Cold Spring, and she quoted my favorite writer. "*I took a walk in the woods and came out taller than the trees.*"

But that's not the Thoreau quote that drives me on. Instead, the one that's been my compass and my guide does. The one about walking toward your dream, and living the life you've imagined.

Mia is the life I've imagined. She's the dream I want to make real.

No more of this surreal stuff. I'm not interested in an in-between state. I can't dwell on moments, and I definitely can't dwell on the past.

The other guy? The one she never loved? I know now he doesn't matter. He has nothing to do with us. What unfolds between Mia and me is between us, and I have it in my power to do everything I can to make sure she's mine.

Starting with telling her how much I want her to be my future. All of it, all of her. Always.

I turn around and head in the direction of the campsite.

26

But finding the right moment to confess my feelings will have to wait until we're off this mountain. Besides, we're surrounded by twenty-five people most of the time.

Two days later, we pack up, ready to say goodbye to both the backpacking and the trip, which ends with a picnic at the inn this afternoon.

I'm itching to say goodbye to this trip. It's been a good one, but boy, do I want it over right the hell now. I need time with only Mia.

On the hike down the mountain, the day is nearly perfect, with beautiful blue skies lined with only a few clouds. The weather app on my phone predicts a few summer showers for later in the day, but honestly, I've never met a summer shower I didn't like. Bring it on.

We stop for photos, and a particularly scenic vista elicits *oohs* and *aahs* from the whole crew. The Sierra Nevada peaks rise majestically in the distance. I suggest a group shot at a large boulder. My phone has been on battery saver mode the whole time, except for morning weather checks, so it still has juice. I turn on the camera and snap a picture. Lisa holds up a finger telling me to wait and grabs a digital camera from her backpack. She's been shooting photos throughout the trip for the company blog. "Take one with mine, too. I'm old school. I like digital cameras better."

I shoot several, and the smiles on all their faces make it clear how much they've enjoyed this adventure tour. They're more ready than before for their next journey together—one that will take them across the country. Maybe that sounds cheesy. Hell, maybe that *is* cheesy. But the way I see it, a little cheese never hurt anyone—a company or a person.

Or a sandwich for that matter.

Which reminds me that I need to introduce Mia to my grilled cheese sandwiches once she's in New York. I have a feeling my hungry jackrabbit will like them.

We wind around switchbacks, cross a small stream, and step over a few fallen branches. When we reach the parking lot, the crew disperses to their vehicles, tossing packs into cars and chatting about showers, picnics, and the move to New York. Lisa closes the trunk then stops in her tracks at the driver's door. A long *ugh* bursts from her mouth as she pats her pockets and unzips all the sections on her backpack.

"I think I forgot my camera," she says, a terribly guilty look on her face.

Mia shakes her head, reassuring her. "No worries. I'll go back and get it."

"I'm pretty sure I left it on the rock where we took

the last photo after Patrick returned it to me. It's not a problem for me to go grab it. You don't have to," Lisa says, taking a step that way.

Mia shoos her to her car. "Go to the inn. Freshen up. I'll get it. That was only twenty minutes back up the trail."

Thirty, to be precise.

Lisa frowns. "You don't have to, Mia."

I pipe in, "I'll go with you, Mia. It's always better to have two on the trails."

"Good plan," she says, then turns to Lisa. "Just save some hot water for me."

Lisa gives her a thumbs-up. "Deal. And thank you."

Mia calls out to the group, "The rest of you go on ahead and get started. We'll be there as soon as we can."

Mia is a chatty bird on the way up, recounting the trip, her favorite moments, and the things her team have said about the tour. She's singing my company's praises, and I couldn't be happier about that, even though I'd rather be talking about us. But she seems to need this, so I do what I sense she most wants—I *listen*.

A half hour later, I spot a shiny black object gleaming in the dirt next to the boulder. Mia snatches it and clutches it to her chest. "Eureka!"

On the way downhill, Mia skips a few steps, turns around, and says, "Want to know what I'm most looking forward to?"

Since this is pretty much the only time we've been alone since she appeared in my tent, I wiggle an eyebrow, and say in a suggestive tone, "What are you most looking forward to?"

I expect her to say something dirty or flirty in return.

Instead, she peers down at her T-shirt, tugging at the neckline, then sniffing it. "A shower."

I laugh. "I'm sure you smell just fine."

She turns around and resumes the downhill trek. "I beg to differ. I haven't had a shower in two days, and I intend to crank up the spray the second we reach the inn. I'd invite you to join me, but then I'd have to fire you."

"Feel free. For a shower with you, I'd gladly get sacked."

"Speaking of showers, that's one thing I'm looking forward to about moving to New York."

"The showers?"

"The water pressure in my building in San Francisco is a trickle." She clears her throat, and her tone shifts, as if she's about to say something serious. "When I look for places in New York, I'm going to have to test the water in every single one."

Finally.

We're finally talking about what happens next.

Good, I need some info. I need to know how far along she is. Where her mind is at. I might be ready to go all in, but there's a difference between putting your heart on the line and putting your heart on the line only to swerve off a bridge and sink to a watery death.

Fine, that's dramatic, but I still need to test the waters about how much to share, and when. Even if

I've pushed Eric from the forefront of my mind, I still don't want to meet his fate. "Have you started the hunt?"

"Yes." Frustration laces her tone, but it's chased by sadness. "It's a nightmare. Nothing feels right, like it could be my home."

"Where are you looking?"

Before she can answer, a clap of thunder echoes like Zeus himself is tossing bolts across the sky. The god, not my cat. We pick up the pace, walking faster around a bend in the trail. Those white clouds? They're a wee bit grayer now.

Mia turns to meet my gaze. There's a new vulnerability in her eyes, something I haven't seen before. "I've been looking in a lot of places. Chelsea. Upper West Side. The Village. Hell's Kitchen. Washington Heights." Her voice is odd, but I can't put my finger on why. It's almost as if she's saying these neighborhoods for the first time, as if she's testing them out as words. Still, there's no Battery Park City in her list.

Time to throw it out there in the mix. See if she bites. "I hear Battery Park City is nice," I say with a wink.

She laughs, but it sounds forced as she marches onward. "That is a great area."

And that response tells me bupkis.

She stuffs her hands in the pockets of her shorts, then takes them out, then jams them back in. "So . . ." Her voice trails off, so I try once more to cast a gentle line and see if she nibbles.

"I like Battery Park City a lot. Do you?"

"Sure." Her tone is even, and I can't read it. "I like it a lot. Definitely."

"Yeah?"

"Yeah. It's great," she says, and my radar is picking up nothing. Zilch.

I reel in the line, and then toss it out once more in a new direction. "Where do you think you'd like to be?"

"Where do you think I should live?" The words tumble out in one fast breath, and I'm not sure where she's coming from. She knows the city well, so I've no clue why she's asking me where to live.

Maybe I can tease out the truth in the guise of humor. I inhale, exhale, and spit it out. "Well, besides the obvious answer that you should live with me, I'd say you're an Upper East Side gal."

She flinches and snaps her gaze at me. Her expression is deadly serious. Her voice is a whisper. "What did you say?"

I've never seen her eyes so intense, so quizzical, and all I can think is I've crossed a line. I've floated a trial balloon that she's not ready for.

Time to reel it in before I drown. "Upper East Side," I say, all casual and no-big-deal cool.

She furrows her brow. "That's what you said?"

I work to sell the cover-up. "Yeah. Sure. That's the obvious answer. That's what I was saying. Upper East Side. Obvious answer."

"Oh." She shakes her head as if she's ridding her ears of water. "I thought—"

"No. That's what I said." My answer is quick and clear.

"Okay, then." She resumes her speedy pace.

Silence covers us for a minute, and once I'm sure I can open my mouth without saying something dumb that scares her the fuck away, I try again. "Anyway, you rattled off a ton of neighborhoods. What kind do you like best?"

She shrugs. "I guess it doesn't matter. I'm even considering Hoboken."

I scoff. "Hoboken? You can't live in New Jersey." Another clap of thunder echoes above us. Her shoulders tense. "We're almost down."

"I'm fine. I'm not scared of rain."

"I know. But it's still better to be out of the weather."

"So, tell me about your disdain for Hoboken. Are you allergic to it?"

"It's just too fucking far," I say. Screw politeness.

"Too far?" She raises an eyebrow. "Does that mean you won't come see me in Hoboken?"

I sigh heavily. "Mia, I was ready to fly clear across the country to see you. Obviously, I'd see you in Hoboken."

"But it's *too far*," she says, imitating me, annoyance coloring her tone.

"It's not too far. It's fine. You should live where you want to live."

"But ideally in a neighborhood more convenient for you?" she says, pointedly, as we round a switchback. I rub the back of my neck, trying to figure out why she's suddenly so combative.

Frustration curls in my chest. The last thing I want

is to argue with her over where she should live. "That's not what I'm saying at all."

She narrows her eyes, and in her won't-back-down stance, I can tell in an instant why Mia runs her own company. She's sweet and kind and savvy, but she also has a lion in her. Sometimes we all need to call on our inner lion. Looks like she's dialing hers up right now. "Then what are you saying, Patrick? Because it's not clear to me at all. It's not *obvious* in the least."

I take a calming breath, marching forward as we argue. I want to stay cool. Hell, I pride myself on being unflappable, but I also want to speak my mind, so I give it one more shot. "I'm saying that I would like you to be closer to me."

"Oh. Is that where I should live? Closer to you? Is that the *obvious answer*?" she fires off at me, sketching air quotes as she spins around—

And stumbles on a rock. She wobbles, and I grab her arm, steadying her. Her breath rushes out in a worried stream. "Shit," she mutters.

"Let's just focus on getting down to the bottom of the trail before the rain starts," I say in a cool tone.

We walk in silence along the trail. As the trees clear and we near the bottom, thunder booms again, and this time it's followed by lightning.

Twenty seconds later, the skies unleash sheets of rain. We're a hundred feet from the parking lot, and Mia takes off running. I run, too, and when we reach the rental SUV, I yank open her door. She looks like a drowned chipmunk. Her hair is matted to her face, and streaks of dirt run down her arms.

"Give me your pack," I say, and when she hands it to me, I shut her door, toss the gear into the back as the water pelts me, and get in the car.

I'm soaked, too. All the way to the bone. I look at her. "I'm sorry, Mia." I take her hand. Squeeze it. "I don't want to fight with you. Ever."

She gives a sigh, the relieved kind. "I'm sorry, too. I think I'm just on edge about the move. I want to do it but everything feels like it's happening all at once. The company, the move, needing a new place." She exhales and speaks softly. "And you. All these changes are coming at me at once."

Foolishly, I hadn't really thought about the fact that Mia is changing everything. Where her business is located. Where she lives. And who she's with— switching from single to involved in the blink of an eye. I should give her the space she needs, rather than crowd her with all these feelings in my heart. "You have a lot on your plate."

"I do, but I ordered this meal. I'm just trying to balance it all."

"What can I do to make it easier for you?" Rain lashes the windshield, and I pull out of the lot at the trailhead.

She shoots me a small smile. "How about you take me to the nearest shower?"

"That I can do."

The rain has other plans. The rain is biblical. The water hurls itself down from the sky. Heavy drops fling at the earth like they're angry at the ground itself.

I focus on driving, slowly ambling along the winding road that takes us away from the trail, staring straight ahead as buckets of water pound the car, punctuated with the *slap-swish* of the wipers.

"This is bad," Mia says. Understatement of the year.

"Yeah, a little more than a summer shower."

I peer ahead. Water gushes over the road in torrents.

My phone buzzes. I glance quickly at the screen to find a flashing triangle.

Warning: Flash flood. Roads closed in the area.

"There's no way to get back to the inn right now," I say heavily. "There's one road out from this trail, and we're on it."

"How long does a flash flood last?"

"Not long, but it usually closes roads for several hours."

She groans, and shoves her hands in her wet hair. She exhales, trying to calm herself, it seems. "Fine. It's not the worst thing in the world. We'll just park and wait it out in your car, right?"

I nearly say yes.

But I don't.

Because the woman wants a shower.

The woman doesn't want to wait in a parked car on the side of the road.

And hell if I'm going to be the schmuck who twiddles his thumbs. I'm the guy who gets shit done. Who gets out of jams. Who fixes the flat tire.

This is one hell of a flat tire in our day.

But I'm going to repair it.

I drum my fingers on the steering wheel. "So, I know a guy who has a cabin..."

27

After I make a call to Carlos, a twisty one-lane road leads up, up, and away from the submerged streets. Mia calls Lisa to let her know we're stuck. From Mia's half of the conversation, I gather that Lisa and the rest of the crew are already at the inn, and she'll check them out and send them back to San Francisco.

Soon, we pull into the driveway of Carlos's cabin on our side of the closed roads.

Heavy rain falls as we dart out of the car and jog to the front porch, where I track down the extra key he said was hidden beneath a bronze miniature Pegasus statue next to a potted fern. I unlock the door and push it open with a loud creak.

Inside, Mia breathes a deep sigh. "It's dry," she says with a wide smile.

"The one time I'm okay with you not being wet." I point to the car. "I'll go get your things. You get in your shower."

"You're my hero," she says, and when I head back

out into the rain, those words make me stand a little taller, walk a little prouder.

Sometimes the hero has to serve up a shower for his woman.

Even if she doesn't want to live in the same place as him yet.

Time. There will be time for that. Time for us to navigate this new relationship road. As I open the back of the car, I remind myself that everything is new for us. We've only ever lived on opposite coasts, and figuring out how to be together will take some adjustments. If she needs to be across the river in Hoboken to make those adjustments, so be it.

I grab her bag, since she'll have another change of clothes in it, and mine, too, then return through the rain to Carlos's sweet digs. It's more like a mountain home away from home, with soft, cushy furniture, a fully stocked kitchen and stainless-steel fridge, a spacious living room with high ceilings, and a fireplace that alone would make the winter trips worthwhile.

The cabin also has a shower.

A shower that's running loud.

And hot.

Starring one very naked woman right now.

I remove my hiking boots and follow the sound of the running water, stripping off my wet, clingy shirt and shorts. The door is ajar, and already steam wafts out.

I knock, but it's purely perfunctory. I'm going in without an invite.

In one quick whoosh, my boxer briefs are off, and I step into the rainfall shower with Mia.

28

Hot, soapy water slides down her breasts, slipping over her belly and gliding across the silver ring in her navel. Her wet hair is lathered thick with shampoo. A trickle of muddy water runs down the drain.

"Told you I was dirty," she says with a wry grin.

I cup her cheek, bending to reach her as she rises on tiptoes. "But I already knew that."

I slam my lips to hers, and we both groan. Her hands shoot to my pecs, slide over my shoulders, and loop around my neck. As for mine, I can't keep them off her tits. I palm those gorgeous beauties as I kiss her hard and fearlessly. I kiss her so she knows how much I want her, how much I need her, and how much I expect her to be the only woman in my arms ever.

Mia dissolves against me, sliding closer, rubbing her hot little body against mine. Water sluices between us, slips down my nose, and glides over my chest.

This kiss is rough and hungry, our teeth clicking together, our lips bruised. She kisses me as fiercely as I kiss her, and I know—no, I *believe*—that the way we kiss says all the things we're not saying.

I need you. I want you. You're mine.

If she's ready to take the next step now, or in six months, or in a year, I'll be fine with it. And because I'm in love with her, I'm going to give her the time she needs. I'm going to be patient with her as she figures us out.

At last, I pull away, my breath coming in jagged pants. "Missed that. I missed that so fucking much."

She tips up her chin. "I missed you."

I arch a questioning brow as my lips quirk up. "Did you?"

"So much," she murmurs, sliding her hand between my legs and grasping my dick. Her eyes light up with mischief. "Sometimes I think you don't realize how much I like you, Patrick."

I can't help but smile. And I can't help but groan as I thrust into her hand as the water streams over us. "Why don't you show me?"

She grips me harder, her hand twisting around my dick as she strokes. "It feels like it's been forever since we've touched, but it's only been thirteen days. And if we were doing the long-distance thing, this is what it would be like."

Desire rattles through my bones. "Like we're going to explode?"

She shakes her head. "No. Like we don't get enough of each other."

"You know that's how I feel. You know that, right?"

"I do."

I shudder on an upstroke, and my brain threatens to short circuit from her touch. "Sometimes I don't think you know how much you affect me."

She brushes her lips to mine in the sweetest, most sensual kiss as she tugs harder. When she pulls away, she says, "Then show me how much I affect you."

She lets go of my cock, spins me around so my back is to the tiled wall, and drops to her knees. Gripping my shaft again, she brings me to her mouth, her eyes sparkling with wild desire as she licks the head.

And I die. Because holy hell. This is heaven. This is another world. This is Mia, on her knees, sucking me off.

Sparks shoot through my body and ripple across my wet skin. As she draws me in deep, she keeps her eyes on me as if she's saying *watch me.*

I grab her head, circling my hands around it. She hums on my dick, and the vibration spreads through my whole damn body. My legs shake, and I have a feeling this won't go down in the record books as the longest blow job. Pleasure slams into me as she flicks her tongue over the head. The sensations are so intense it's like an onslaught of euphoria. Shockwaves of desire rocket through me with her every touch.

"Mia," I groan, my eyes floating closed.

She stops, and I fall from her mouth as she demands, "Watch me."

I blink open my eyes and pull her closer. "Get back on me."

She pumps her fist down my shaft, working me over, licking the tip.

"You're going to kill me, aren't you?"

She shakes her head, smiling wickedly. "No, but I want to blow your mind." She toys with me using tight, teasing strokes.

"Take me in," I tell her, my voice rough. "Please."

"Are you sure?"

"Mia," I say, as if in warning.

"Tell me what you want, Patrick."

"You," I groan, frustration and desire seeping into my voice in equal measure. "You, all the time. You, around the clock. You with me always. You. Fucking you. And right now, I want your lips on my dick."

With a wildly satisfied grin, she gives me the relief I seek, wrapping her lips nice and tight around me. She takes me so deep I hit the back of her throat. "Christ, Mia. You know why this is so good?" I ask, as sheer bliss threatens to obliterate my brain.

She shakes her head. I grip her tighter, my fingers digging through her hair as the water pounds us both.

"Because it's you doing this to me," I say, and her eyes blaze. "It's you I'm looking at. It's all you."

One more suck. One more thrust into her throat. One more moment of holding her gaze. That's all I can take. I don't even try to fight it off. The orgasm rips through me as I come in her throat with a growl.

My climax erases the world, the cabin, the entire day. All I'm aware of is the intensity of the aftershocks as they spread to every molecule, until Mia stretches and rises, wedging her body against me.

I open my eyes and grasp her tight, hold her close.

As I come down from the high, she takes the soap, rubs it on her hands, and washes my arms, my chest, my abs.

God, how I love her.

She runs a soapy fist down my dick, and it tickles.

I laugh.

I love her so fucking much.

I take the soap from her and turn her around, rinsing the remnants of shampoo from her hair, then spreading conditioner in, and washing her arms, legs, belly, and breasts. By the time I'm done washing off the conditioner, she has sparkly skin and probably the cleanest tits in the world.

I take her face in my hands and breathe out hard. She looks up at me, her eyes big and vulnerable. "Is that how I affect you?"

I swallow hard, shake my head.

A crease appears in her brow. "It's not?"

I run my finger down the line in her forehead. "Sometimes, maybe most of the time, I don't think you realize that I'm completely in love with you."

She melts into my arms, her soft, naked body pressed to mine. Her lips part, but she says nothing, and I'm not sure why. But then, she turns the shower off, and a lone tear streaks from her eye.

29

"Are you sad?"

She shakes her head, and her smile is radiant. "No. I'm happy. I'm so happy because I'm so in love with you."

And this—this feeling, like I can do anything, like the world is shaded with bright, bold colors, like I'm living inside a hit song I can't stop singing along to—is happiness. It's joy. It's love, and my heart feels like it doesn't even fit inside my chest anymore.

"I'm in love with you," I say, and then, because it's out there, I can't stop. "I'm so wildly in love with you, Mia."

She loops her arms tighter around me. "I'm so in love with you, but I thought you didn't feel the same."

My jaw drops. "What?"

She nods. "I thought it was one-sided."

"You thought I wasn't into you?"

"Well, I knew you liked me. I didn't think you were in as deep as I was."

I grab her ass. "Mia Summers, if there's one thing you can be certain of, it's that I'm in so deep with you, it's beyond over my head."

I grab a towel and dry her off.

She shoots me a quizzical stare. "You're not just saying that because you liked the blow job?"

I scoff as I grab another towel and run it over my body. "Let me prove to you that this has never been just sex. It'll never be just sex. I've always made love to you, and I'm going to do that right now. So you know how you affect me. So you understand when I say it's you I want, you every day, I mean every single day and every damn night."

I hang up the towel, scoop her into my arms, and leave the steamy bathroom. I glance down the hall and make our way to one of the bedrooms. I kick open the door, and a king-size bed with a white cover awaits. I carry her, lower her onto it, and watch as she scoots up the bed to the pillows.

I join her, grabbing her waist and flopping down on my back. "Come sit on my face."

She shudders. "Really?"

"You say that like you think I don't want to eat you right now."

"I thought you were going to make love to me."

"I am. First with my mouth. Then with my whole body." I grab her hips, but I don't need to convince her anymore. She crawls up me, and lowers herself to my face, and I kiss her wetness. I close my eyes, groaning instantly. The very second I taste that silky heat, I'm roaring inside.

And she's moaning.

And rocking.

And grinding.

My Mia gets into it. Oh hell, does she get into it. It doesn't take her long to find her rhythm. Grabbing the headboard, she circles her hips. I hold her tight, moving her across my mouth, flicking my tongue over her swollen flesh, rubbing my stubble all over her.

She pants, and moans, and cries out.

Then, she turns wild. She's a woman possessed, riding my face, fucking my mouth, grinding and rocking until she shudders, and everything goes silent for one gloriously suspended moment when she doesn't move.

Then, her shoulders shake. Her belly tightens. Her thighs grip my head.

And she is nothing but *oh God, oh God, oh God, oh God.*

She comes on my lips, trembling against me. I keep my grip on her until her moans subside, then I gently move her off and slide her down the bed, flipping her onto her belly. She's a warm, soft creature now, all blissed-out and sex-drunk.

I yank up her hips, so she's on all fours, resting on her elbows.

"You're going to make love to me like this?"

I nod. "Let me show you how I can make your favorite position feel even better."

With her hips raised, I line up my cock at her entrance. Then I slide inside, and I groan. I shudder. It's just so fucking intense. Her back bows, and she moans, then looks back at me.

I thrust deep in her, her heat gripping me as her intense eyes stay on mine.

When I'm all the way in, I band an arm around her waist, and tug her up so she's kneeling with me. Her back is against my chest, her body so tight to mine.

I raise one hand to her face, turning her so her lips meet mine. And we kiss, and we groan, and we fuck. She lifts her arms, wrapping them behind her, around the back of my head. My hand slinks between her legs, and she shivers against me.

I show her how her favorite position can be even more intimate, how it can bring us even closer. I don't stop kissing her, not when she cries out, not when her breath turns ragged, and not when she trembles.

When she starts to fall away from me, I hold her even tighter, letting go of her lips at last so she can cry out her pleasure as she comes on me. And that's all I need to join her on the other side of the cliff.

30

<hr>

She traces lazy lines down my chest.

I'm smiling.

I don't think I can stop.

This woman. She does this to me.

I dot a kiss to her forehead and tug her closer in the crook of my arm. "I want this every day. I meant what I said in the shower. I want you every day."

"Me, too."

I stroke a hand through her still-damp hair. "I'm so happy you're coming to New York, Mia. You have to know, it's my greatest dream come true. You and me together in the same zip code." I'm not worried anymore about saying too much. This cabin unlocked my heart, and my mouth right along with it. I need her to know she's everything to me. Patience is great and all, but sometimes you have to unleash the truth.

She turns and levels me with her gaze. "Remember at your place when you asked if you were part of my decision?"

I nod.

She nods, too. "You are."

And that organ in my chest is hula-hooping right now. I can't hold back any longer. My plan to take some time has gone up in smoke. *See you later, patience.* I run the backs of my fingers over her cheek. "I don't want you to move to Hoboken. Or Chelsea, or the Upper East Side."

She arches a brow. "Oh, you don't? Why's that?"

Nerves swoop down, but just as quickly, they fly away. "I would think the obvious answer is"—I let those words from earlier linger before I give them a whole new meaning—"that I want you to move in with me."

She gasps, and her eyes widen. "You do?" She speaks in a hushed whisper.

"Yes. I want to go to bed with you, and I want to wake up with you. I want to make you grilled cheese sandwiches for lunch on a lazy Saturday afternoon and then curl up with you on the couch and not watch sports since we'll be too busy getting naked. I want to say goodbye to you when you leave for work in the morning, and I want to text you during the day asking if I can bring you home anything. I want to share a closet with you and watch you rub that coconut lotion on your legs in the morning after you get out of the shower, and then pick up the towel you used and send it to the laundry with mine."

Her eyes shine with tears, and her lips quiver with happiness. "I don't really understand how you made damp towels sound romantic, but somehow, you did."

I run my thumb over her top lip. "I know your

fears. I know your hopes and dreams. I know your heart. I love you. Will you live with me? Will you make my home yours, too, and let me love you every single day?"

All the hope in the world hangs in the balance, suspended in this brief moment before she answers. But I don't let myself worry, nor do I fear that I'm scaring her away. Because when you know you're madly in love with someone, you don't want to keep it to yourself any longer. I need her to know she means everything to me.

She nods, and a tear slides down her cheek. She inches closer, dusting my lips with the sweetest kiss any woman has given any man. "I've wanted you to ask me since the day I told you."

I blink. "What?"

"When I told you I was moving to New York. And you asked if it was because of us."

I shoot her a look. "You said, 'It's not as if I expect you to ask me to move in and marry you.'"

She smiles. "I know what I said. I also know what I meant."

I laugh. "Woman, if you wanted to live with me, you should have said something. I'm not a mind reader."

Her fingers travel up my belly. "I think I needed you to come to it on your own terms." She winks. "I would think that's obvious."

"Feel free to hit me over the head with this obvious stuff, Mia. Want to know why?"

She smirks. "Why?"

I tap my chest. "Because sometimes—hell, maybe a

lot of the time—I'm going to need some help decoding."

"Fair enough," she concedes, then she nudges my shoulder. "But there was no way I was going to tell you that day that I wanted all of you. Hello? That's a recipe for scaring a guy away."

I bring her closer in my arms and kiss her forehead. "I was afraid I'd scare you away if I told you then that I wanted you with me."

"You wanted the same thing then, too?"

I shrug happily. "I think so. Yeah, the idea was just starting to form, but this trip with you solidified it."

She hums a note of approval. "So, my corporate retreat was good for you, too . . ." She sounds quite pleased with herself.

"Yes, Mia. The guide learned something, too."

She climbs on top of me, laying her naked body on mine, propping her chin in her hands, and looking at me. "So all the wilderness made you realize you wanted me?"

"It did."

"You're so outdoorsy," she says with a laugh.

I wiggle an eyebrow. "Turns out you are, too."

"Hmm. Maybe I am."

"You are," I say firmly.

A smile crosses her lips. "Fine, you're right. I'm into this whole nature thing with you. And I still want to do it in a tent."

"Don't even worry about that, Mia. That can happen anytime. Tonight, if you want."

Naughtiness twinkles in her eyes, then she sighs

happily and inches forward to kiss me. "I wanted to tell you in your tent the other night how I felt."

"I wanted to hear it."

"But I also didn't want to say anything sooner because this is all kind of new for me."

I furrow my brow. "What do you mean?"

"I've never really been in love before. Not like this, where I can feel it everywhere."

I feel like Zeus on catnip. This woman makes me so high, makes me feel so good. "You've never felt like this?"

She shakes her head. "Have you?"

I shake mine, too. "No. I feel like you're a part of me."

She brings her lips to mine. "I am." Then she kisses me, and it's so tender, so gentle, I swear I'm floating.

When we separate, she speaks first. "It's different between us, you know that, right?" The look in her eyes is intense and meaningful.

"How are we different?"

"I think you were worried the same thing would happen, but this isn't the same. What I feel for you has never been the same as anything else. The reason I held back for so long was I was worried you didn't feel the same way about me."

I scoff. "As if that's possible."

She taps her fingers on my chest. "And I was concerned that if it was just a short-term thing for you, that you and Max would have a falling out. I didn't want that to happen to him again."

And with brilliant clarity, I can see her warning to

me was never a warning about her heart. It was because she loves that big lug of a brother.

I run my hand up her arm. "Max and I won't have a falling out, because I'm not letting you go," I say, finally telling her what I wanted to say many nights ago.

It's funny, in a way, that so much of falling madly in love comes down to when you find the guts to speak your whole truth. But men and women aren't always ready to bare their souls. Instead, we sidestep the hard stuff, we avoid tough conversations. That's human nature – we can't always solve every problem when it happens, even if we want to. Sometimes we don't yet have the tools, or the guts. We have to hike through the woods, march up the hills, climb over rocks, before we come out on the other side.

That's where I am now. That's where we are. Finally saying what we've both wanted to say for a long time. The best part is learning she's wanted the same things all along.

When she pulls back, a thoughtful look passes over her eyes. "I should tell Max I'm moving into the building. I should also tell him not to worry that he'll lose you as a friend, since I have you wrapped around my finger." Her eyes twinkle as she holds up her pinkie.

"Definitely tell him you're moving in with me. But I did let him know we were seeing each other. I actually told him the night you left New York."

She laughs. "Did he freak out?"

I shake my head. "Not entirely. But I think he'll be happier now, especially since he'll be able to see more of you this way."

"That makes me happy, too."

"I suppose I'll need to break the news to Zeus that he won't have me to himself much longer," I tease.

"Oh, sweetie. I think the cat already knows."

"You do?"

"I bet that cat knows everything."

"Yeah, you're probably right."

Her stomach rumbles, and I rub my hand on it. "Hey, hungry monkey, I mentioned grilled cheese sandwiches earlier, and I bet you like them."

Her hazel eyes turn to saucers. "I love them."

I smack her ass. "I had a feeling you would. Carlos told me he had groceries sent earlier this week since he'd been planning to come up, but he didn't make it. I bet I can find all the fixings for a sandwich for you."

Fifteen minutes later, I serve her a deliciously gooey Gouda cheese on sourdough, and she tells me it's the best thing she's ever had. I think she might be exaggerating, but I don't care. I eat up her compliment as I grill a sandwich for myself.

As I cook, she clears her throat and adopts an overly professional tone. "By the way, even though the trip has ended and all, I suppose I should officially fire you."

I look at her over my shoulder as I flip the sandwich. "And I've never been so happy to be sacked."

When mine is done, I stand across from her at the counter and take a bite of my sandwich. "Damn, I sure can make a mean grilled cheese."

"Sandwich master. I'll add that to your list of attributes." She puts her sandwich down. "Hey, what do I call you now? Are you my roomie? My boyfriend? My lover? My trail guide? A god in bed?"

I point in the air, as if I'm selecting that option. "Last one. Clearly."

She rolls her eyes. "Seriously."

"You want to know what to label us?"

"I do work in the beauty business. We label everything. So, what are you?"

I lean across the counter, brush a crumb from her lips, and press a soft kiss to her mouth. "Yours."

31

———

The next twenty-one days pass in a flurry and slog. The days are fast, filled with details and arrangements, but the nights are slow, marked by longing.

I count down the hours until I can spend them with her.

We talk and text and Skype, and the Skype sessions are both fantastic and completely unsatisfying, since I want to be the one giving her the orgasms, not her vibrator. But hey, at least it's something.

I learn even more about Mia during those three weeks before she moves. One night on the phone, she warns me that she has a thing for blankets, and loves to snuggle under many soft, fleecy ones at bedtime. I tell her I'm all for a top sheet and leaving the windows open. She shudders and says *brrr*.

"I'll change my habits for you," I tell her.

"Or we'll compromise."

"That works, too."

"But I might have bought a new adorable fleece

blanket for the couch that I couldn't resist. It should arrive in two days. I hope you don't mind."

I smile. "Mia, you can decorate your house however you want."

"Great. I have some posters of Chris Hemsworth as Thor arriving the day after."

"Except that way."

I learn, too, that she likes to sleep in on weekends, but she also wants to go for runs and bike rides with me. I'm an early riser, so I tell her I'll go solo on Saturdays and later in the day with her on Sundays.

"Or we can just have sex all morning on weekends," she offers.

"That works for me. In fact, you can consider me a yes anytime you want to fuck."

She laughs. "Good to know. Oh, and I think I feel the same way, too."

"Think? You think?"

"Well, you're kind of well-endowed, Patrick. A woman sometimes needs a break so she can walk straight."

And that goes down as my favorite compliment ever, even more than the grilled cheese.

Obviously.

We make plans, too. Dates we want to go on in Manhattan. I tell her I'm taking her to the Brooklyn Botanic Gardens, and to Governors Island, and to any bath and beauty shop she wants.

"Stop being so perfect. You're making me look bad," she teases.

I laugh. "I'm not perfect. Just normal."

"As a thank you for being so normal, I'll take you on a date to REI."

"Don't get me excited."

"And we'll go back to the trail in Cold Spring."

"Now I'm even more excited."

"And I'll walk your cat with you any time you want."

"Mia," I chide. "He's our cat now."

The other plan we make is for me to help her move. She's hired a company to transport some boxes and a few items of furniture, and I offer to join her in San Francisco to help handle that before we fly to New York together.

"You'd do that for me?"

"Mia, you're moving your company and yourself across the country. I'll take a few days off to help you move. It's what any good *god in bed* would do."

Soon, but not soon enough, I've crossed off twenty days on the calendar. On the twenty-first day, I wake up early, harness my cat, and take him to one of my favorite trails outside Manhattan. That's when I realize how right Mia was about cats.

32

Conversations with the Cat
   Zeus

Along the trail, the cat sniffed leaves, darted after birds, and stood lookout on the canoe as he and the man enjoyed an hour on the water. The sun shone brightly in the big blue sky, warming his lush fur with so much heat, he purred his appreciation for the great outdoors.

He was a simple cat. Give him some fish, a spot of sunshine, and his favorite person, and he was good to go.

Sometimes, though, he also liked bugs.

Tasty creatures. Crunchy and savory at the same time. Such a wonderful combination.

The hunter in him kept his eyes peeled for his favorite flavor—something the man had called moth. Back on the trail, a winged insect had the good fortune to zip too close to him. In one fast lunge, Zeus sprang forward, caught it, and crunched into the snack.

He considered playing with it. Batting a paw to it. Torturing it. Bringing it home to share with the calico lady he'd been getting to know.

Quite well, in fact.

But today, Zeus opted for instant gratification and devoured the moth.

The man laughed. "Sometimes you just have to go for it, right, buddy?"

The moth went down easily. So satisfying.

The man stopped in his tracks, tugging on Zeus's leash. He looked up at him, wondering what had prompted him to pause. "Meow?"

"Don't you think, Zeus? This is one of those times, isn't it?"

Zeus asked again. "Meow?"

The man talked and talked as they clambered down the hill, and Zeus curled up on the front seat of the Jeep, pleased that he had once again proven why he was a most excellent companion.

Then, he slept. After all, he'd only slept ten hours so far that day. And he needed fifteen for his beauty routine.

33

With my duffel on my shoulder, I stop by to see Max.

His eyes register surprise as we talk, but then he claps me on the shoulder, and wishes me luck. My flight leaves in two hours, so I don't have much time. But that's where my life-hacking skills come into play.

Or my simple, go-with-what-you-have skills, really.

At Kennedy airport, I zoom past security thanks to TSA PreCheck, then I do something I rarely do at airports. I shop. I pop into a specialty shop then a gourmet store. As I buckle up on the plane, I call my sister, and she shrieks so loudly I have to pull my phone away from my ear. After an endless flight across the country, I finish my commerce at San Francisco Airport, settling for a photo since the store is closed. I catch a Lyft to Mia's apartment in the heart of the city and wait for her to buzz me up. My duffel is on my shoulder, and I carry a plastic bag with all the items I've bought on the way.

I'm hopped up on nerves and excitement, adrenaline and possibility. I'm not sure I'm fully prepared for what I'm going to do, but I also know that preparation isn't what matters.

This is a spur-of-the-moment decision, and sometimes the best things in life happen that way.

When Mia opens the door, I drop my bag, cup her cheeks, and look into those eyes I love. Eyes I've missed. Big, beautiful hazel eyes. "Let's make a stop on the way to New York."

She raises an eyebrow. "A stop where?"

"Vegas."

She blinks. "You don't even like Vegas."

"I know. But I don't want to play the slots or see a show. I want to marry you. I want you to walk into our apartment in New York as my wife."

Her jaw comes unhinged. I watch her as she swallows then tries to speak again.

I don't pressure her. I wait.

Finally, her voice nearly cracking, she asks, "Are you serious?"

"Do you really think I would joke?"

She shakes her head. "No."

"Is that a no?" I ask, but I'm honestly not scared. I know deep inside, in the marrow of my bones, that this woman will be my wife. That doesn't make me cocky. That doesn't make me overconfident. It just means I believe in our love. I believe in it so heartily that I'm not afraid.

"It's not a no. I'm just shocked. I didn't expect this."

"That's okay. I didn't, either. But then I went for a walk in the woods with Zeus this morning, and I knew it was time to go for it. I had an epiphany, you could say. Like what happened to you a month and a half ago in New York," I say, reminding her of the day she decided to begin changing her life. A faint smile creeps across her face. "And everything was clear. Sometimes in life you just have to go for what you want."

"Yeah, you do," she says, her dimples appearing. That smile makes me press on.

I hold up a finger. "But just so you know that I'm not a schmuck who'd propose empty-handed, I did a little shopping."

A laugh bursts from her lips. I'm not sure if it's from surprise or shock. She hasn't said yes yet, but that won't stop me from diving into my impromptu proposal.

I dip into the bag and take out a small royal-blue box. Her eyes are drawn to it, like lasers. "It's not a ring. I want you to have the ring you want. But the jewelry store at JFK did have this adorable bunny necklace."

Laughing, she clasps her hand to her mouth as I click open the box. A small silver pendant of a rabbit rests on the velvet. "I can't ask you to marry me without some kind of jewelry. So for you, Jackrabbit, a bunny seemed perfect. And I can take you shopping tomorrow at Katherine's in the city if you'd like."

She starts to speak, but I press my finger to her lips. "Don't answer yet."

I hand her the box, and she takes it, clutching it tight. She doesn't speak, but she smiles so wildly it's like she can't even contain it.

That grin is magic to me.

"And then there's this," I say, fishing around for the

item I picked up at the gourmet shop. A bag of Marcona almonds. "Since I know you'll get hungry, and I want you to know I'll always be thinking of you."

"I will, and I love that you're thinking of my belly and me."

My heart thumps hard. "One last thing. The day we went to Cold Spring, you mentioned a magnet store at the San Francisco Airport."

"You remember that?" she asks, wonder in her tone.

"When the woman you love tells you things, you listen." I tap the side of my head. "You store it up here. You never know when it might come in handy. Now, since it's ten p.m., the store is closed, but you said you never shopped there anyway, just stopped to read the quotes. And tonight, this one reminded me of you." The corner of my lips curves up, and I shrug hopefully. "And maybe, of you and me."

"Show me," she says as I reach for my phone. Her voice is a whisper now, but in it I hear hope. I have faith she wants the same things that I do.

Sliding my thumb over the screen, I find the magnet I snapped a picture of. "Bear in mind, this isn't some great philosopher's quote. This isn't from one of the writers I studied in my lit classes. In fact, I'm not even sure anyone knows who said this. But it seemed the most fitting quote of all."

I show her a magnet with four simple words on it:

Why the hell not?

And she cracks up. Her hands fly to her belly as she laughs. "Oh my God. Are you seriously proposing to me with a bunny necklace, some nuts, and a pic that says *'Why the hell not?'*"

I square my shoulders and give her my honest answer. "Yes. I am. This isn't complicated. It's simple. I don't need to weigh this. There's no need for a pros-and-cons list. Marrying you is all *pro*. I have no doubts. I have no questions. My only hope is that you'll say yes." I run my thumb along her jaw, and she leans into me. Then I whisper, "But if you're not ready, I'll wait for you. I'll wait until you're ready, whenever that is."

She raises her chin, her eyes locked on mine. "You'd wait for me?"

"Yes."

"Even if I'm not ready?"

My answer is truthful. "I'll wait as long as it takes."

She wiggles an eyebrow. "So, like, say, a day?"

I grin wildly. "Is that a yes?"

She sets all the goodies inside her apartment, then she loops her arms around my neck, rises up on her tiptoes, and kisses me softly. "It's a *why the hell not?*"

Then she tugs me into her place, kicks the door closed, and kisses the hell out of me.

I lift her up, wrap her legs around me, and spin her against the wall.

She's laughing and smiling and kissing and beaming. "I've always liked surprises, but this is the best one ever."

And she kisses me more.

"I never pictured us getting married in Vegas," she says, when she takes a break from kissing me.

"Wait. Does that mean you pictured us getting married?"

She rolls her eyes. "Of course I've pictured us getting married."

I kiss her neck then meet her eyes. "And what did you picture?"

"I saw us getting married on a hillside at sunset."

"That's what you imagined?"

She nods. "The rest was a blur. The only part that mattered was that it was you and me."

Mia and me. That's what the rest of the night feels like—a blur of her and me.

34

She's right. All that does matter is the *who*. But color, cut, clarity, and carats are pretty important, too. Sometimes in life, you can streamline. You can simplify. You can lean on a life hack.

Choosing an engagement ring is not one of those times.

As promised, the next morning I arrange to take her to Katherine's in Union Square, but first we have details to tend to.

As Mia showers, a burly man with a beard knocks on the door, and he's flanked by a redheaded dude with tattoos down his arms. "Hey there. You're here for the couch and stuff?"

"Yep. Salvation Army."

I let them in and help them lift then carry the sofa down to their truck full of donations. The next item to go is her desk, along with a coffee table. I help them carry boxes of books, cookware, and other items that are on their way to a second life. She already donated her car to the ASPCA.

I thank the guys, give them a tip, and head upstairs to Mia's increasingly empty apartment. She stands in the middle of the tiny living room, eating the almonds and scanning the place where she's lived since she started Pure Beauty in her kitchen with an idea, a vision, and a business plan.

"Will you miss it?"

"Probably," she says, a tinge of sadness in her sweet voice.

"That makes sense. It would be strange not to."

"I have a lot of fond memories of this city. This whole coast. But I also know I'm going where I want to be."

"And you don't mind ditching so much of your stuff?" I ask her for probably the twelfth time.

"I don't need two couches. I don't need two beds. All I need is to add a metric ton of pillows to yours and I'll be good to go," she says, not for the first time since we discussed this idea.

"Good. As long as you're sure," I say.

She meets my gaze across all the space in her home and taps her finger against her lip. "Let's see. In exchange for stuff, I get new pillows, access to one brother in the city, another in the building, and the master sandwich maker in the same home. I'm okay saying goodbye to a little thing known as a couch." Then she walks to me, sets the bag of almonds down on her purse, and presses her hands to my chest. "Also, now I have twenty-four-hour access to my own personal mover anytime I need something heavy lifted."

"That is, indeed, one of the perks of living with me." I shake my head, amused at my own faux pas. "I'm sorry, Mrs. Almost-Milligan. I meant to say that's one of the perks of being married to me."

And an hour later, I introduce her to another one of the perks.

Ring shopping.

Since Spencer's family owns Katherine's, which has locations around the world, he arranged for the store manager in San Francisco to personally assist us in picking a ring and sizing it today. Mia takes her time, trying on as many rings as she wants.

She shows them all to me. "I really don't know what to look for."

"You didn't imagine what you might want when you helped Max and Chase pick rings?"

She shakes her head. "No. I swear. I wasn't thinking of anything but what Henley and Josie would want." She takes a beat. "Which is kind of funny, since I was definitely completely into you when I was helping Max pick out the ring."

"And you never fantasized about what you'd want?"

She leans in close and brings her mouth to mine. "All my fantasies about you were of the bedroom variety."

I growl my appreciation under my breath. "Be sure to share all your fantasies with me, but right now, let's keep looking."

The helpful brunette manager brings her more

rings. Mia tries many on, and when she slides an emerald-cut ring onto her finger, my phone buzzes with my sister's text tone.

Evie: HOW IS IT GOING? ARE YOU RING SHOPPING? DID SHE PICK? DYING TO KNOW. SIMPLY DYING.

Patrick: She's trying on the whole store. It's adorable.

Evie: GAH. I WISH I WERE THERE.

I stuff my phone in my pocket as Mia shows me another solitaire.

"What do you think?" she asks.

"Mia, I think they're all beautiful. Because they're on you."

She narrows her eyes, then glances at the manager. "He's no help," she says playfully.

The woman laughs and then holds up one finger as an assistant scurries over to her. "Just one moment."

She steps away from us to chat with her employee, then rejoins us to tell us she has one more ring she thinks might be perfect.

Mia shrugs happily. "I'd love to see this perfect ring."

"One moment," the manager says, then heads to

another side of the display case, roots around amid all the gleaming diamonds, and returns a minute later. "I think you might like this one, Ms. Summers."

When Mia slides on the ring, she gasps. "I think this is the one," she whispers reverently. "Can I take a picture and show your sister?"

"I assure you there's nothing Evie would like more than to be a part of this."

"Wait. Did she know you were going to propose?"

I rub my knuckles against my ear. "I have the pierced eardrum to prove it," I say, then tell her about Evie's excited reaction when I called her while we were taxiing for takeoff yesterday.

I snap a photo and send it to my sister.

Patrick: Mia loves this ring. She wants to know if you approve.

I look at my bride-to-be. "Now, we wait."

But not for long. Ten seconds later, my phone beeps.

Evie: I BOW DOWN TO THAT STUNNING TWO-CARAT ART DECO-STYLE VINTAGE RING THAT I JUST PICKED OUT FOR YOUR BRIDE!!!!

I laugh and show Mia the message.

"Your sister picked this out?"

"Evidently."

Mia turns to the manager, question marks in her eyes.

The brunette's eyes twinkle. "My associate just received a phone call from an Evie Milligan, recommending we show you this ring."

Mia's smile is one I will remember for all time. "Sisters always know best."

Then, we choose two platinum bands and opt to have them engraved.

* * *

The next morning, the movers arrive, and they pack up Mia's remaining items. The head mover tells us the boxes should be at the destination in Battery Park City in seven days.

I grab her suitcases and my duffel bag as she locks the door behind her. For a moment, she simply stares at the door, then she takes a breath and turns around.

"Are you good?"

"So good."

"Are you sure?"

"I'm positive."

She drops the key with the landlord, blows a kiss to her building, and then threads her fingers through mine. "I am so good with everything."

We pick up the bands and the resized engagement ring, and catch a flight to Vegas.

35

"You bought me a suit?"

She bounces on her toes. "Yes!"

"Why on earth would you buy me a suit?"

She parks her hands on her hips and stares daggers at me in our room at the Luxe, a hotel run by one of Evie's good friends.

"Patrick, do you have any idea how handsome you look in a suit?"

I shake my head. "Oddly enough, I do not."

"You're stunning. I happen to be a big fan of you in a suit, and you're going to marry me in a suit. That's just the way it goes."

"But will it fit?"

She rolls her eyes. "Kangaroo, where there's a will, there's a way. That same sister who picked my ring also went to your apartment and snagged your suit measurements for me. She helped me find a tailor here in Vegas, and he made sure it would fit you. I had it sent to the hotel, and the rest is going down in quickie wedding history."

And so, I put on the charcoal suit my bride chose for me, while she slips into a simple, shimmery white dress that stops at her knees. The bunny necklace rests on the soft skin of her neck. Her diamond ring gleams on her hand.

On her feet are flats. "I don't care if I'm a foot shorter than you. I'm not hiking up a hill in heels."

And that's another reason why I love this woman. She likes simple solutions.

With our marriage license in hand—that is one thing I do love about this city, you can get a marriage license with a snap of your fingers—we climb into the limo that picks us up at our hotel. It's part of the wedding package I ordered. The car whisks us away to Red Rocks Canyon, on the horizon west of Vegas.

There, we walk along a trail, framed by rust-red cliffs and rocks, and meet the officiant. His name is Walker, he wears a black suit and a white shirt, and his glasses slide down the bridge of his nose.

The sun hangs low in the sky, its bright peach and fiery-orange rays signaling the coming sunset.

Walker clears his throat. "We are gathered here today to join Patrick and Mia in holy matrimony."

Since this is a simple ceremony, he slides right into the vows. "Do you, Patrick, take Mia to be your wife?"

With my gaze locked to hers, I give the easiest answer ever. "I do."

"Do you promise to love, honor, cherish, and

protect her, forsaking all others and holding only unto her?"

"I do."

Walker looks to Mia. "Do you, Mia, take Patrick to be your husband?"

Her smile can't be contained. "I do."

"Do you promise to love, honor, cherish, and protect him, forsaking all others and holding only unto him?"

"I do."

And I soar. I am officially the happiest man in the world.

"It is now time for the exchanging of the rings."

From my suit pocket, I take out the platinum bands from a small velvet bag and hold up hers. "I promise to love you, cherish you, hold your hand on balconies, take care of you whenever you need me, and hold you from this day forward, until death do us part," I say, and Mia's eyes well with tears as I slide the band on her finger.

She takes mine. "I promise to love you, cherish you, hold your hand over bridges, take care of you whenever you need me, and hold you from this day forward, until death do us part."

She puts the ring on my finger.

"You may kiss the bride."

And so I do, kissing her sweet lips, cherishing her taste, loving that as the sun sets over the cliffs, this woman is now my wife.

Later that night, I make love to her, and it just gets better and better every single time.

When she curls up against me for our first night together as husband and wife, I hold her hand, studying our rings.

"I love our rings," she says, snuggling against me.

"The best part is what's engraved."

She laughs and dots a kiss on my nose. "That is the best part of these rings."

After all, it says what's always been true.

The cat knew first.

EPILOGUE

A few months later

"And then you need to bring caviar for the cat."

Camilla laughs at my final tip. "What would any glamping feline need but caviar?"

Zeus stretches a paw across my leg, and raises his chin at the WRBC Channel 10 anchor. He's become a regular on the *Tips and Tricks for Enjoying the Great Outdoors* segment. Turns out when you're a hiking cat, you're in demand. The first segment with him was one of the station's most popular, so they asked if I could bring him back for each and every one.

Gladly.

He's one chill feline, and if he helps more people and pets enjoy the world around them, then I'm a happy camper.

And Camilla says she'll be a happy glamper if she follows my tips.

"I know you'll have a great time, Camilla."

"I'll report back on whether my curling iron works in the woods." Then she turns to the camera. "And that's all for today. Join us next week for another segment from our outdoors expert and his cat, Zeus."

Camilla thanks me again, shakes my hand, and tells me she'll see me next week.

I load Zeus into his pack and head home.

To see my wife.

Since it's Friday morning, she's just finished her shower and is rubbing coconut lotion into her shapely legs when I return to our place.

"Ah, just like I imagined," I say, then press a kiss to her cheek.

After she tugs on her skirt and zips it up, she tosses me her damp towel. "And now for my fantasy."

"Laundry," I say in a deliberately husky tone, as I drop it into the basket I'll be sending out later today.

"Mmm. You get me so excited when you talk about chores. Tell me more about the household tasks you'll engage in."

I loop my arms around her waist, and press a kiss to the back of her soft neck. "I'll order some groceries," I say seductively.

"Oh yeah," she hums.

"I'll pay the utility bill."

She cries out, as if in pleasure.

"I'll even pick up a gift for Max's wedding."

She laughs and slides around in my arms so she's facing me. "Silly kangaroo, I already did that."

"I have no doubt you did."

Then she slips away, puts on a blouse, and blow-dries her hair. When she's done, she tells me she's leaving for the office.

"Same here," I say. I give Zeus a goodbye scratch on the chin, and we take off together.

Mia heads for the Pure Beauty offices, and I head to meet Dana to review our upcoming trips. Dana handles Pure Beauty's regular excursions now, and that works out just fine. In fact, everything has worked out just fine.

Sure, Mia and I argue every now and then. Like last week, when she wanted to give me head before I went down on her. Insistent little thing, she was sure she'd win.

She didn't.

I can be pretty convincing with my tongue.

There was another time we didn't see eye-to-eye, but she was right on that count. It turned out that fresh strawberries and champagne did make a better gift for my sister's engagement party than my idea to give them a backpack. In my defense, my sister didn't have one, and I still don't understand how anyone can function without one.

In any case, I let Mia pick a gift for her brother's wedding. Besides, I've been the recipient of the greatest gift of all. Not just Mia, obviously. But the gift of teasing Max relentlessly about the fact that I beat him in the marriage game. He's the last of our crew to tie the knot, even though he was engaged well before I started seeing his sister.

But hey, every man goes at his own pace.

Some just go a little faster than others when they fall in love.

That's evidently the kind of guy I am.

The next night, Mia is a radiant bridesmaid as she stands across from me at the front of the ballroom in the Plaza Hotel while Henley and Max exchange their vows.

The venue was Henley's choice. She works on cars all day long, so she needed nothing less than a full Plaza wedding, and that's what she's having.

Chase and Josie are part of the wedding party, too, while Spencer, Nick, and Wyatt are parked in the front rows with their wives and kids. Spencer and Charlotte's son is adorable, perched in his mom's lap, with blond hair to match hers. Nick holds his infant son, who has blue eyes the same color as Harper's. Wyatt's toddler daughter holds his hand.

Briefly, I wonder when Chase and Josie will head down that path, but there is plenty of time for that.

When the officiant tells Max he can kiss the bride, Henley jumps in his arms then smothers him in kisses.

They have the right idea, so once they're walking the other way down the aisle, I give my wife a kiss.

She smiles and sighs happily. "Everyone's married off now. Does that mean the rest of us have to get knocked up soon, too?"

I tense for a moment. "Is that your way of telling me you're pregnant?"

She laughs and shakes her head. "No. But the abject terror in your eyes is all I need to keep taking my birth control."

I grab her hand tighter, tug her in closer. "I'm not scared. You just caught me off guard. Do you want to have kids soon?"

"Maybe not today, and maybe not tomorrow, but someday. Someday is soon enough."

"That sounds good to me, too."

Then we join our friends and family, and when I dance with Mia later that night, I remember the last time I danced with her at a wedding, when I was ready to fly clear across the country to date her long distance. Now, several months later, she's here with me every night.

I run a finger across a strand of her hair. "Sometimes, I think this life we have is everything I imagined. But then I realize, it's even better than I could have dreamed."

"Me, too."

ANOTHER EPILOGUE

A little after that

By now, most women have met enough players, enough guys who don't ever want to settle down. I suppose that's fine. There's a time and a place for everyone.

As for me, I knew what I wanted from the first night I met Mia. I wanted her, and for more than one night.

But you don't always get what you want just because you're ready for it. Even though I like to think I'm easy-going, laid-back—hell, even *normal*—I discovered I had my own baggage.

I had to let go of what I thought I needed—proximity—before I could get it.

I needed to be willing to take what I could get. When I fell in love with Mia, the problem I had to solve was learning that she was worth the distance, worth the miles, worth the wait.

Now I have everything I could ever have imagined

and then some. Sometimes, you just have to say *why the hell not?* and go after the life you want to lead.

That's what I have now. A great job, fantastic friends, a healthy family, a cat who isn't like any other cat, and a woman I've pitched my tent with.

Speaking of tents, I've made good on my promise to introduce Mia to the true joys of camping. We've spent many nights under the Milky Way, and I make sure she always sees stars.

If you catch my drift.

After all, we both like camping best . . . with our particular *style*.

AND ONE MORE EPILOGUE

Sometime soon enough

Conversations with the Cat
   Zeus

He padded toward the bathroom on the quietest feet in the home. The woman had gone in there the second she woke, springing out of bed.

She never bolted up in the morning. Perhaps she needed to stroke his soft fur to feel better about whatever was making her nervous. He'd sensed her nerves. He was talented like that.

Now, as the man slept deeply, Zeus nudged his shoulder against the ajar door, pushing it open.

The woman was perched on the toilet bowl, holding a stick. He cocked his head to the side, watching her. She stretched her arm to push the door closed.

"Shh. I don't want him to know I'm even taking this."

Zeus parked his rear on the tile and stared at her, while she stared at the stick.

Tick tock.

She set the stick on the sink and flushed. She watched the stick more as she washed her hands.

Zeus never looked away from her.

At last, she peered at the stick once more. She gasped.

She dropped down to him, scooped him up in her arms, and pressed her lips to his furry face. "You're going to be a big brother."

Then she set him down and burst out of the bathroom, waving the stick and waking up the man, who erupted into the kind of cheer that Zeus could only assume accompanied a fresh can of tuna.

Whatever was exciting the man and the woman, he found great satisfaction in the fact that he had known first.

MIA'S EPILOGUE

Mia

Some years later...

Look, it's still sexy when my husband does the laundry. Especially since there's so much of it. Twins will do that though. Audrey and Whitney are busy little girls who have a way of making messes out of everything. Their clothes, the couch, the cat. Zeus's tail was collateral damage in a marathon fingerpainting session last week. But that boy didn't seem to mind – he is so good with the kiddos. He let them paint his tail a sparkly green. He's always been a patient cat – more like a dog, in some ways if you ask me. But, lest anyone think Zeus is purr-fect, he was a little ornery when I washed the green paint off his tail. Hey, I get it. If I had a tail that spectacular, I'd be particular about it too. But I explained to him that I was using Pure Beauty, and since my company just launched a line of cruelty-free pet shampoos I like to think he appreciated my choice.

As for me, I appreciate my sexy, kind, funny and caring husband. Patrick works hard with his adventure tour business, and I work hard with mine, and at night, he still works me hard. Just the way I like it – sometimes at home here in New York, and sometimes when we go camping together in the summer.

When we do that, Chase and Josie and Max and Henley watch our girls. They all have their own kids now, so we trade off with the babysitting duties. All in all, I love living in New York and seeing my family here, as well as all the new friends I've made, like Bellamy Hart. Even though I found my Happily Ever After, I get a kick out of her dating advice show A Million Frogs. It's fun to catch up with her and hear what it's like to brave the romance waters in Manhattan these days....and I'm particularly interested in getting all the details of a "sort of date," her words, that she went on last night. Apparently, she went to a costume party at Spencer's bar, and she met a guy there who might very well be her match. When I grab a slice of cake with her the next day, she tells me the guy is Spencer's cousin, Easton Ford...who's known for throwing elite romance matchmaking parties in Manhattan. So exclusive, you need a special invite. Color me intrigued. But Bellamy plans to crash one of his parties next weekend. I can't wait to hear what happens when she does. For now, I've got my best friend to go home to every night.

* * *

Eager for more from the Big Rock world? Meet

Spencer's cousin, Easton Ford, in COME AGAIN a sexy, enemies-to-lovers romance FREE IN KU!
Binge the entire Big Rock series now in KU!
Big Rock: Spencer & Charlotte
Mister O: Nick & Harper
Well Hung: Wyatt & Natalie
Full Package: Chase & Josie
Joy Ride: Max & Henley
Hard Wood: Patrick & Mia

BE A LOVELY

Want to be the first to know of sales, new releases, special deals and giveaways? Sign up for my newsletter today!

Want to be part of a fun, feel-good place to talk about books and romance, and get sneak peeks of covers and advance copies of my books? Be a Lovely!

ACKNOWLEDGMENTS

Thank you to Helen Williams for knowing exactly what to do with the fantastic photo and bringing it to abalicious life on the cover. Thank you to KP Simmon for the strategy and support on everything. Thank you to Kelley, Candi and Keyanna for the day to day work that is so vital. Thank you to Michelle for ALL THE BOOKS.

On the editorial side, I am fortunate to lean on Lauren Clarke, Kim Bias, Dena Marie and Jen McCoy for story shaping, and to Virginia, Tiffany, Karen, Marion, Janice for their keen eyes. Big shout to Jen, who's been my sounding board for all six of these books!

As always, I am grateful to many fellow authors for their daily guidance, support and friendship including Lili Valente, CD Reiss, Laurelin Paige, K. Bromberg and Marie Force. Thank you to my family for putting up with me. Big kisses to all my dogs.

Most of all, I am thankful every day for all my readers. You are a joy!

I've written more than 100 books! **All of these titles below are FREE in Kindle Unlimited!**

The Love and Hockey Series

<u>The Boyfriend Goal</u>

A roommates-to-lovers, teammate's little sister hockey romance!

<u>The Romance Line</u>

An enemies-to-lovers, player and the publicist, forbidden romance!

<u>The Proposal Play</u>

A brother's best friend/marriage of convenience romance!

The Girlfriend Zone

A coach's daughter romance!

The Overtime Kiss!

A single dad/nanny romance!

The Flirting Game!

A neighbors to lovers, fake dating romance!

Hockey Ever After

Just Breaking the Rules!

A brother's best friend/workplace/one who got away romance!

Just Playing for Keeps!

A grumpy sunshine, fake dating romance!

Darling Springs

It Seemed Like a Good Idea!

An only one-bed-in-the-room, forbidden, small town bodyguard romance!

I've Got a Crush On You!

A grumpy sunshine, workplace romance where the boss has a secret identity!

Holiday Romances

Merry Little Kissmas

Fake dating my brother's best friend at Christmas!

My Favorite Holidate

Fake dating the billionaire boss at Christmas!

The My Hockey Romance Series

Hockey, spice, shenanigans and cute dogs in this series of standalones! Because when you get screwed over, make it a double or even a triple!

Karma is two hockey boyfriends and sometimes three!

Double Pucked

A sexy, outrageous MFM hockey romantic comedy!

Puck Yes

A fake marriage, spicy MFM hockey rom com!

Thoroughly Pucked!

A brother's best friends +runaway bride, spicy MFM hockey rom com!

Well and Truly Pucked

A friends-to-lovers forced proximity why-choose hockey rom com!

The Virgin Society Series

Meet the Virgin Society – great friends who'd do anything for each other. Indulge in these forbidden, emotionally-charged, and wildly sexy age-gap romances!

The RSVP

The Tryst

The Tease

The Dating Games Series

A fun, sexy romantic comedy series about friends in the city and their dating mishaps!

The Virgin Next Door

Two A Day

The Good Guy Challenge

How To Date Series

Friends who are like family. Chances to learn how to date again. Standalone romantic comedies full of love, sex and meet-cute shenanigans.

My So-Called Love Life

Plays Well With Others

The Almost Romantic

The Accidental Dating Experiment

A romantic comedy adventure standalone

A Real Good Bad Thing

Boyfriend Material

Four fabulous heroines. Four outrageous proposals. Four chances at love in this sexy rom-com series!

Asking For a Friend

Sex and Other Shiny Objects

One Night Stand-In

Overnight Service

Big Rock Series

My #1 New York Times Bestselling sexy as sin, irreverent, male-POV romantic comedy!

Big Rock

Mister O

Well Hung

Full Package

Joy Ride

Happy Endings Series

Romance starts with a bang in this series of standalones following a group of friends seeking and avoiding love!

Come Again

Shut Up and Kiss Me

Kismet

My Single-Versary

Ballers And Babes

Sexy sports romance standalones guaranteed to make
you hot!

Most Valuable Playboy

Most Likely to Score

A Wild Card Kiss

Rules of Love Series

Athlete, virgins and weddings!

The Virgin Rule Book

The Virgin Game Plan

The Virgin Replay

The Virgin Scorecard

The Extravagant Series

Bodyguards, billionaires and hoteliers in this sexy, high-
stakes series of standalones!

One Night Only

One Exquisite Touch

My One-Week Husband

The Guys Who Got Away Series

Friends in New York City and California fall in love in this fun
and hot rom-com series!

Birthday Suit

Dear Sexy Ex-Boyfriend

The What If Guy

Thanks for Last Night

The Dream Guy Next Door

Always Satisfied Series

A group of friends in New York City find love and laughter in this series of sexy standalones!

Satisfaction Guaranteed

Never Have I Ever

Instant Gratification

PS It's Always Been You

The Gift Series

An after dark series of standalones! Explore your fantasies!

The Engagement Gift

The Virgin Gift

The Decadent Gift

The Heartbreakers Series

Three brothers. Three rockers. Three standalone sexy romantic comedies.

Once Upon a Real Good Time

Once Upon a Sure Thing

Once Upon a Wild Fling

Sinful Men

A high-stakes, high-octane, sexy-as-sin romantic suspense series!

My Sinful Nights

My Sinful Desire

My Sinful Longing

My Sinful Love

My Sinful Temptation

From Paris With Love

Swoony, sweeping romances set in Paris!

Wanderlust

Part-Time Lover

One Love Series

A group of friends in New York falls in love one by one in this sexy rom-com series!

The Sexy One

The Hot One

The Knocked Up Plan

Come As You Are

Lucky In Love Series

A small town romance full of heat and blue collar heroes and sexy heroines!

Best Laid Plans

The Feel Good Factor

Nobody Does It Better

Unzipped

No Regrets

An angsty, sexy, emotional, new adult trilogy about one young couple fighting to break free of their pasts!

The Start of Us

The Thrill of It

Every Second With You

The Caught Up in Love Series

A group of friends finds love!

The Pretending Plot

The Dating Proposal

The Second Chance Plan

The Private Rehearsal

Seductive Nights Series

A high heat series full of danger and spice!

Night After Night

After This Night

One More Night

A Wildly Seductive Night

Joy Delivered Duet

A high-heat, wickedly sexy series of standalones that will set your sheets on fire!

Nights With Him

Forbidden Nights

Unbreak My Heart

A standalone second chance emotional roller coaster of a romance

The Muse

A magical realism romance set in Paris

Good Love Series of sexy rom-coms co-written with Lili Valente!

I also write MM romance under the name L. Blakely!

Hopelessly Bromantic Duet (MM)

Roomies to lovers to enemies to fake boyfriends

Hopelessly Bromantic

Here Comes My Man

Men of Summer Series (MM)

Two baseball players on the same team fall in love in a forbidden romance spanning five epic years

Scoring With Him

Winning With Him

All In With Him

MM Standalone Novels

A Guy Walks Into My Bar

The Bromance Zone

One Time Only

The Best Men (Co-written with Sarina Bowen)

Winner Takes All Series (MM)

A series of emotionally-charged and irresistibly sexy standalone MM sports romances!

The Boyfriend Comeback

Turn Me On

A Very Filthy Game

Limited Edition Husband

Manhandled

If you want a personalized recommendation, email me at laurenblakelybooks@gmail.com!

CONTACT

I love hearing from readers! You can find me on Twitter at LaurenBlakely3, Instagram, or Facebook at LaurenBlakelyBooks, or online at LaurenBlakely.com. You can also email me at laurenblakelybooks@ gmail.com

www.ingramcontent.com/pod-product-compliance
Lightning Source LLC
Chambersburg PA
CBHW032244310726
48973CB00008B/2284